SHERLOCK HOLMES: THE RUSSIAN CONNECTION AND OTHER NEW ADVENTURES

Fans of Sherlock Holmes will find much to treasure in this elegantly written anthology of ten brand-new adventures. The inimitable Sherlock Holmes and his trusty companion Doctor Watson are back once again in N. M. Scott's third collection of stories inspired by Arthur Conan Doyle's classic crime-busting duo.

Dip into Watson's case notes and discover how a man came to be found suspended in an ice block in Victoria Park, what happened when an infernal locomotive ran amok in Moscow, and how a severed foot pointed the way to a grisly murder.

Sherlock Holmes: The Russian Connection And Other New Adventures

by

N. M. Scott

Magna Large Print Books
Long Preston, North Yorkshire,
BD23 4ND, England.

British Library Cataloguing in Publication Data.

Scott, N. M.
Sherlock Holmes:
the Russian connection and other new adventures

A catalogue record of this book is
available from the British Library

ISBN 978-0-7505-4215-9

First published in Great Britain in 2013 by The Book Guild Ltd.

Cover illustration by arrangement with
The Book Guild Publishing

Published in Large Print 2016 by arrangement with
Book Guild Publishing

Magna Large Print is an imprint of Library Magna Books Ltd.

Printed and bound in Great Britain by
T.J. (International) Ltd., Cornwall, PL28 8RW

For
Janet & Rog

Contents

1

The Russian Connection

I was putting pen to paper, glancing over my old notes one rainy morning in October, when I realised my colleague Mr Sherlock Holmes had for the last hour at least been staring morosely into the fire, scraping aimlessly away at his violin upon his knee, unable to exert his considerable mental faculties on some problem concerning criminality.

My companion did not own a university degree, but nonetheless was possessed of a most remarkably keen and probing intellect which might readily be aligned to the research scientist, for his formidable knowledge of both forensic pathology and chemistry should have put many an Oxon or Cambs undergrad to shame.

I was thus gratified when footfalls upon the stair and a somewhat constrained knock at the door announced our visitor.

My companion laid his violin aside and sprang up from his armchair, snatching his old black clay and matches from the mantelpiece. It was as though a charge of electricity had shocked his torpid system into activity. Perhaps, like I did, he sensed that the imposing individual stood before us not only represented a period of consulting work, which had been sadly lacking in the previous fortnight, but a somewhat generous fee in the offing.

'Sir Pelham-Stillitoe, do sit down. A cigarette or cigar? Perhaps a cup of coffee?'

'Coffee would be most kind, but I shall on this occasion abstain from smoking, if you don't mind. But please, gentlemen, I do not abhor strong tobacco. Charge your pipes, by all means.'

Sir Pelham reminded me of Lord Melbourne, in appearance at least. His fine, aquiline nose, grizzled side whiskers, greying locks of longish hair swept to one side, the handsome, still youthful face, the wonderfully poised attitude and immaculate attention to every aspect of his grooming, spoke to me of a man self-assured, taking his rightful place in the highest echelons of polite society. He was a very wealthy and upstanding personage, one of the most popular and clubbable men in London, and yet I confess, despite his outward show of propriety and vigour, he seemed to me desperately melancholy behind the confident facade.

'Mr Holmes,' said he, 'I am a recently bereaved widower and since the death of my dear wife I find myself plagued by approaches from women of a certain age seeking romance and matrimony. It seems I am suddenly popular with ladies at every turn.'

'And the fact that you are still hale and hearty at seven and sixty, you are a prominent member of London society and own properties in Mayfair and a substantial country park in Hertfordshire, must surely weigh heavily in your favour.'

'Yes, you would imagine I owned a carefree life of glittering parties, country house weekends, huntin' 'n' fishing and visiting my Pall Mall clubs. Yet I must tell you, sir, that I am presently in dire difficulties, my reputation on the brink of ruin and derision on account of a wretched block of apartments in Clerkenwell. Number thirty-two, Desborough Mansions, to be exact.'

The rain was lashing incessantly against the pane, and whilst I peered languidly from my desk at the wet, shiny grey slates of the roofs opposite, I confess I felt a good deal of sympathy for this English gentleman who, for perhaps the first time in a long and distinguished life, now found himself in a stormy sea foundering upon the rocky outcrops of ruination.

'Sir Pelham, obviously a block of apartments in itself is harmless enough, but Clerkenwell, if I may say so, is a rather surprising down-at-heel locale for a discreet assignation. I would venture to suggest a woman is involved?'

'Indeed, a Miss Svetlana Sergeyev. If only I had not taken a recommendation from a dear acquaintance of mine at my club, none of this should have happened.'

'Please do not take offence, Sir Pelham, but presumably you sought this lady out for company – or else...'

'Nothing improper whatever occurred,' he insisted. 'Our relationship was at all times wholly chaste, and it pains me to say this but over a period of months I grew to love Svetlana dearly. How can I convey to you the atmosphere of our intimate candlelit suppers, the iced vodka, saffron rice, salted fish and soured cream, tender skewered lamb, smoking a Montecristo cigar while gazing into her beautiful eyes, alert to her every whim and pleasure. How wonderfully conducive to my spirits she was. Alas, we were not alone, never entirely alone.'

'You have received a compromising letter, I take it. My dear Pelham, both Doctor Watson and I have dealt with similar cases in the past. You now find yourself the owner of – how shall we put it – a delicately fused time bomb primed and ready to explode, and you would rather prefer it didn't. This is perfectly natural. May I see the letter?'

'Here, take it.'

The elderly gentleman passed the epistle across as though it were tainted with acid and he could hardly bear to conceal his revulsion at its contents.

My Dear Sir Pelham-Stillitoe,
Svetlana Sergeyev was the recipient of many of your kindnesses and love kisses, soothing your tears on her bosom, listening to you spill your heart out while she prepared tea, pouring the boiling water from the samovar. A discreet pat on her knee, an intimate glance.

Alas, dear sir nothing in this world is free. Every assignation at her apartment in Desborough Mansions was carefully observed from a spyhole by myself, Mr Salt, and a valued and trusted friend of mine, Mr Pepper, who is in fact a most popular Fleet Street journalist who writes a column and articles for many of the serious broadsheets you yourself no doubt peruse over the breakfast table.

For every assignation, Miss Svetlana Sergeyev and her business associates charge at an ascending rate. Six thousand guineas each for the first three meetings, ten thousand guineas for all consecutive visits, which we calculate to the number of ten. Therefore, multiply ten thousand by ten and add six thousand multiplied by three and you have a final figure. Our accountants inform us a Coutts cheque will not be required, rather Bank of England notes to the same value.

If you fail to comply, Reuters wire print service and The Times, The Pall Mall Gazette *and* The Telegraph *and many low-life dailies shall be running off the print presses by the end of the week, emblazoned upon every front page the impossibly abominable headlines 'Most unbecoming of a much respected public figure, the recently widowed Sir Pelham-Stillitoe takes Russian mistress Svetlana Sergeyev. A sordid nest of forbidden love revealed.'*

Await further instructions.

Yours,

Mr Salt

The old fellow ran his fingers through his silvery grey hair and sighed.

'Mr Holmes, I am blessed with a couple of delightful daughters. Well brought up, loving and wholly doting on their father.'

'You naturally wish to avoid scandal,' said I, leaving my desk and wandering over to the coal scuttle to pick out a cigar.

'But there is a deeper problem.'

'And that is?' asked Holmes, recharging his clay.

'I am in love with Svetlana. I adore her, despite the letter.'

'She is but one part of a gang,' said I, 'no more than a variety girl, an actress playing a part.'

'What you have fallen in love with, Sir Pelham,

is a mirage,' said Holmes in disbelief. 'You yourself are merely a source of money, a financial consideration, a means of raising capital. Do you not understand that?'

'I know all this, gentlemen,' he said, slamming his fist hard against the arm of the chair in frustration. 'Listen, all I am requesting is that you look after my little Svetlana, that no harm will come to her. Destroy this Salt and Pepper gang, by all means. I am probably but one of their unfortunate victims. I will pay you a generous fee, Mr Holmes. You are a consulting detective of justified and enormous reputation. Is it too much to ask, protecting this lovely Russian woman from the courts and prison, allowing her at least another chance?'

Perhaps the discerning reader of this narrative will forgive me for advancing the pecuniary cause. Upon this occasion the fee won. Holmes agreed the lady should avoid prosecution and he would instead concentrate his considerable energies on bringing Mr Salt and Mr Pepper, and other gang members, to justice. However, it must be mentioned, criminal cells operating in London are difficult to deal with – often ruthless, violent and highly organised.

'Well,' said I after our visitor had left, 'should we fail, Holmes, Sir Pelham shall require a first-rate legal firm and all of his considerable influence in places of government to stay the rabid hounds of Fleet Street if this ever gets out. The conspiring journalist Mr Pepper shall no doubt run riot with his pen.'

'The national press in this country cannot quite so easily be gagged, Watson. Even the lofty proprietors are a fickle crowd. The ensuing scandal concerning Number Thirty-two Desborough Mansions would be bound to shift a vast circulation of newspapers, particularly amongst the "low-life" dailies, whereupon beckons a vast amount of dividend for shareholders. Also, it could be argued this Svetlana Sergeyev might indeed be a woman capable of hurtling a normally respectable, wholly moral gentleman into the depths of untold depravity, Sir Pelham-Stillitoe but a willing participant, a slave if you will. Mr Pepper shall sell his story widely.'

'Sir Pelham was not being entirely honest with us, you infer?'

'I am of an open mind, Watson. Anyhow, our illusive Mr Salt will no doubt contact Sir Pelham-Stillitoe with directions as to how the blackmail money is to be lodged. Then we can make inroads and break their operation. Incidentally, the gang shall have moved on from Clerkenwell and found a new safe address. Number Thirty-two Desborough Mansions will surely be "old hat" by now.'

'Pointless checking there, then.'

'Indeed. Might I suggest instead, my dear Watson, we revisit "Violinland" and enjoy an afternoon of Paganini at St James's Hall, followed by lunch at Marcini's.'

After our concert we took the subterranean railway from Piccadilly Circus, looking forward to a splendid lunch at an Italian restaurant. Joining us in the compartment was a fellow I recognised who had been sitting near the front at St James's

Hall, clapping and shouting at the end of the performance.

'I've got a shop in north Lunnon, don't you know. I am an unabashed devotee of model trains. As with armaments, the Germans, God bless the Kaiser, are the world leaders at present. Are either of you gentlemen model railway enthusiasts, perchance?'

'An expensive hobby,' said I, leaning back upon the cloth-covered seat, smoking my cigarette. 'More for the wealthy grown-up chap than the bonny child.'

'I grant you it is an expensive pastime. Perhaps one day England shall develop its own unique little miniature rolling stock but for the present the German manufacturers are "it", sir. None can beat them for detailed engineering and fine metal casting. Are either of you up for a demonstration?'

'Certainly,' answered Holmes, warming to our music-loving fellow passenger. 'North London, you say. Whereabouts is this shop of yours?'

'Highgate, along the High Street and next to the bank. You can't miss it. How it gladdens my heart that gentlemen such as yourselves should show such obvious delight in little railways. Ah, I get out here. The demonstration is at noon tomorrow. Here is my card. I look forward to seeing you both then.' We watched him hurry off along the platform and then our rail cars pulled out.

'What a delightful chap,' said I. 'What does his card say, Holmes?'

'P. Jenner, Rodwells Model Shop, Thirty-nine The High Street, Highgate. Specialists in German cast metal and printed tin locomotive stock and accessories.'

When he flipped the card over, however, my companion's face froze in horror. I myself felt a painful restriction around my heart.

'Good gracious, Holmes,' I gasped, peering over.

Bring the money owed. A Gladstone bag of bank notes, otherwise Sir Pelham-Stillitoe shall be wrecked and ruined by the end of this week. Yours ever, Mr Salt.

'He must have been following us about.'

'Just so, dear boy, this entire gang employed watching our every move. The money represents a fortune and they will not hesitate to murder for it. P. Jenner of Highgate it is, then – tomorrow noon.'

Our arrival the following day in Highgate was heralded by an absolute downpour of sheeting rain. We were caught without umbrellas in freezing cold gusts that whipped up the puddles and sent rainwater slewing off shop awnings and running along the gutters. Both Holmes and I, within five minutes, were soaked to the skin, our clothes damp and soggy. Bedraggled and miserable, we trudged along the High Street, sloshing along the wet pavement, toiling in first one direction and then the other, past the Gatehouse public house, the school, the bank, but still no sign of a model railway shop did we encounter. No. 39 did not exist. We tried at the post office and even a constable of police could not help.

'Rodwells Model Shop – never heard of it.' He watched us warily, sneering at our pathetic drowned condition.

'It must be one of those confounded riddles,' I told Holmes. 'Is there a dastardly code involved?'

Holmes's dour countenance brightened when I mentioned this.

'Very well, old chap, we'll turn thirty-nine on its head and see what we've got.'

'Ninety-three,' I replied, stating the obvious.

We crossed over the road and it turned out that No. 93 was an undertaker's, a very prosperous and respectable looking establishment. H. Parr & Son. We were thus surprised to see a sheet of paper, a notice adhering to the plate glass window.

Demise of P Jenner of Highgate. Donations, wreaths and flowers at this sad time appreciated. Burial at noon at West Cemetery. Funeral tea to follow.

'The cemetery. So Mr Salt guides our every move. Have you your service revolver close to hand, Watson? We are in the deepest danger. This handover has been planned with meticulous care. Will we meet the attractive Russian lady Svetlana Sergeyev, I wonder, before they shoot us in the back?'

Once inside the gates, the old overgrown West Cemetery looked resplendent with its huge vaults and eerie statuary. Above us an overcast sky of dull pewter did not exactly bode well for our endeavours. Upon entering through an archway flanked by Egyptian pillars known as 'The Gateway to the City of the Dead', we proceeded to trudge along the wet and dripping funerary avenue that sloped gently upwards to an area of the cemetery known as 'The Circle of Lebanon', where there grew before us an enormous cedar. I clutched my service revolver and felt my shoulders tense.

'Put the bag over here,' I heard the voice of a foreigner say. 'Place it carefully at the base of the tree and scram. We are armed and fully prepared to counter any nonsense should the need arise, which I'm sure it won't. Please convey to Sir Pelham our good wishes and to his pretty daughters, Edith and Anne, also.'

We saw the Gladstone bag snatched by a short, squat fellow wearing a trawler man's oilskin cape with concealing hood. He reminded me of an India rubber monk.

'Wait one second,' said Sherlock Holmes, leaning on his swordstick cane, as cool as a prince. 'Is there a receipt? This is a proper transaction, I take it, between gentlemen.'

'Are you mad, you stupid, arrogant Englishman?' a voice shouted. 'Now get out of here, the pair of you, or I'll deliver you both to The City of the Dead, free of charge. They're quite expensive, these fancy plots round here.'

Another, much taller individual, himself wrapped up in oilskins, came out from behind a monstrous granite, ivy-wreathed vault and pointed a machine pistol in our direction.

'Ha, a notable firearm favoured by the Tsarist secret police. I am pleased to make your acquaintance, comrade Yeugeny. You defected to London in 1898, I believe, and now choose to live in the capital and play for high stakes blackmail. The Foreign Office is my brother Mycroft's domain and you are unaware he keeps me always informed of émigrés.'

'Abratna, abratna,' called the shorter man sternly. 'He wants to rile you, Nicolai, the devil. Let's shoot this pair of blustering oafs and have done with it.'

'A receipt,' Holmes demanded with equal annoyance. 'You have your money, Mr Salt, the least you could do is have the decency to offer us a signed piece of paper.'

I knew from both Holmes's evasive stance and his flashing eyes that we were about to be shot at. Recalling my army training in Afghanistan, I knelt down and let off a quick volley. The taller fellow clutched his chest and fell backwards. Crashing against the granite vault he rolled over on his side, shivering and convulsing, until he lay still, his machine pistol some way distant.

Holmes meanwhile slung his cane like a javelin at the shorter of the pair and managed to disable him. The swordstick must have struck the thigh, causing profuse bleeding, but, alas, the fellow got away, using the maze of paths dividing the West Cemetery to good advantage.

Back at our diggings all was far from sweetness and light. A sombre mood of repressed anger prevailed. Sir Pelham-Stillitoe paced up and down in front of the hearth like a caged beast.

'My blackmail money – all gone.'

'I'm afraid so. Of course, I'm sure it could eventually be recovered but you shall require the assistance of Scotland Yard. I'm sorry, Sir Pelham, but there you are, the Russian escaped. He eluded us.'

'I cannot believe what I am hearing. The greatest consulting detective, a man of immense talent and infinite brain resources, cannot simply keep track of a bag full of money. Your friend shot this ex-Tsarist secret policeman, Nicolai Yeugeny, after all. By gad, sir, I should have thought you would have cleared this matter up by now. Instead I find Mr Pepper is still at large and wielding his poison pen. Am I yet to be destroyed by an avalanche of Fleet Street detritus, sir?'

'I'll forgo my fee,' said my friend irritably. There was an unmistakable steeliness about Holmes.

'It's despicable, you of all people.'

'Forgive me, Sir Pelham,' replied my companion, puffing furiously on his long cherry-wood pipe and growing redder in the face, trying to control his rising anger. 'Doctor Watson and I were facing two extremely ruthless and well-armed opponents who had the advantage of ample cover and a well-planned strategy.'

There was a knock at the door. Mrs Hudson the housekeeper popped her head round.

'A Lady Marchmount to see you, Mr Holmes. You and Doctor Watson were apparently responsible for saving her pet spaniel Albert in Kensington last week. She has come specially to see you.'

'Oh, for God's sake, show her in,' said Holmes, looking flustered. 'Only for a minute or two, mind, for I must redouble my efforts on Sir Pelham's behalf to trace his dratted Gladstone bag. Watson, be a good fellow and pour us all a stiff whisky, will you. Who the devil is this Lady Marchmount, anyhow?'

A little blonde woman, so petite and pretty, stepped inside our rooms, her silky ankles divine and her crinoline flouncy dress of the latest Parisian haute couture, fitted tightly round from shoulder to hips. She thrust her dainty bosom forward, smiling sweetly.

'Albert is so much improved, thank you gentlemen. I took Doctor Watson's advice and fed him his deworming powders. Do excuse me while I get out my purse. A guinea was the fee and it is money well spent.'

'Deworming powders?' I muttered incredulously, wondering who on earth Lady Marchmount had mistaken me for. I was certain I had never seen her before in my life.

But then the truth emerged. From her purse she drew a machine pistol of the type used by the ex-Tsarist policeman and émigré Nicolai Yeugeny and, lifting the catch with surprising dexterity, she took aim and prepared to fire directly at Holmes's head. *We are finished,* I thought.

'Miss Sergeyev. Svetlana,' Sir Pelham-Stillitoe pleaded, falling to his knees. 'Don't shoot Mr Holmes, don't do it, my darling. I love you. Let the rest of the blackmailers go hang, we can elope to Finland, get out of Europe altogether, begin life anew. You shall be my Russian princess and want for nothing.'

The young woman hesitated at first, in two minds, undecided whether to pull the trigger, but she eventually relented. I swear I thought in those few seconds of indecision, Holmes and I were about to die, to be fatally wounded in our own rooms at Baker Street.

'You really love me?' she demanded coquettishly.

'Of course I do, darling. I can't live without you.

I have the means and the influence. I am well regarded in diplomatic circles and can easily obtain the necessary travel permits. Might a large and comfortable dacha just outside Moscow suit your new life of wealth and privilege, my dearest?'

'I like this very much, my little fluffy chick,' she cooed, kicking the gun beneath the couch and joining him over by the door, smothering his face in wet kisses. 'All the time I loved only you,' she insisted.

'Of course you did, Svetlana, of course you did. I never doubted it.' Sir Pelham paused to compose himself.

'Will you give us a few hours, my dear Holmes? Allow us to leave the country unhindered.'

'You have my word,' said Holmes, with a slight bow. After all, he had just narrowly avoided being assassinated.

That evening I was sitting in my armchair basking in the warm, cheery glow from the fire, listening while that infernal rain lashed down Baker Street, when I heard a carriage draw up outside our diggings. Holmes was nursing a slight cold, no doubt brought on by the sound soaking we both received earlier at Highgate Village.

'Lestrade,' he remarked listlessly, peering out of our bay window. 'Not a good night to be out working on a case. By Jove, I'm shivering and going down with a chill, Watson!'

'Easy on the cough mixture,' said I. 'A couple of teaspoons is all it takes to relieve the chest. I've examined you and you must go to bed. Cover up and stay warm. A dratted bore for a man like you,

but there we are.'
'Bother,' said my companion. 'Where are the matches?'
'You're not smoking,' said I, 'your lungs shall become congested.'
Our bickering was interrupted when Inspector Lestrade entered the room, tut-tutting, chewing upon his bottom lip. 'Most peculiar I'm sure, can't make it out,' he muttered.
'What can't you make out?' asked Holmes, lighting his cigarette and coughing.
'Geoffrey James of *The Pall Mall Gazette* is dead.'
'So what, only a journo,' said I, striking a match and lighting my own cigar.
'Well, actually he was a highly rated journalist, Doctor Watson. A war and later political correspondent, he contributed to *Tit-Bits, Answers* and *Pearson Weekly*. A long career saw him lunch with the likes of Henry Irving, Disraeli and Lord Palmerston. One of Fleet Street's finest. He shall be sadly missed, but it's the nature of his death that bothers us at the Yard, I'm afraid to say.'
'Suspicious?'
'I think so.'
'Go on.'
'Well, he was recognised as having visited Westminster Abbey earlier this afternoon arm in arm with a pretty young lady, fair-haired.'
I shuddered. Holmes's shoulders tensed up. Could this woman possibly be the Russian Miss Svetlana Sergeyev?
'They strolled into the sanctuary and the North Ambulatory as tourists are wont to do, Mr James explaining to her, a foreigner evidently, the

monuments to Francis Vere and Elizabeth Nightingale, acting as her guide, if you will.'

'Get to the point, Lestrade,' Holmes cut in irritably.

'Well, later Geoffrey James was found by the verger with his brains blown out, slumped in Edward the First's ancient, graffiti-covered coronation chair, a decrepit oak throne dating from around 1300 and brought out for every coronation since 1308. Blood all over the place, there was, but no sign of this mysterious blonde woman.'

2

The Ladies' Cycle Club

Before perusing this narrative concerning a curious case which occurred in the year 1887, during a short sojourn to Pulborough in West Sussex, it must be said independent young lady cyclists in that era still experienced disapproval from more conventional individuals and sometimes had caps thrown at them, or else were greeted with sneers and derision on the road. Attitudes, of course, have changed but back then a bicyclist was someone new and daring.

I recall one afternoon we were walking up by the church with our friend Mr Phelps, when Holmes and I noticed a group of young lady cyclists approaching the timber lychgate. They glided to a halt, dismounted and primly walked their bicycles up the road towards us, a flame-haired girl with a freckled nose and sun-tinted face striding ahead. They looked anxious about something so we hurried across to see if we could be of assistance.

'Is perchance one of you gentlemen a Mr Sherlock Holmes, the consulting detective?' asked the pretty red-headed girl, wheeling her bicycle over to the churchyard wall.

'I am he,' said my companion, stepping forward and shaking her delicately gloved hand.

'Oh, thank goodness. We were told by Mrs Lawson who owns the holiday let that you and Doctor Watson were up from London. We are in desperate need of your opinion,' said she breathlessly.

'Do go on.'

'It's that old duffer Carlton up at the manor. The major hates us like billy-o for using his footpath to ride our bicycles along, and he's complained to the village committee that we never ring our bells properly and that we startled his damned stupid little pooch. Yapping and snarling and biting at our ankles, it was, that's more like the truth!' she said hurriedly, her apple blossom cheeks flushing delightfully.

'Is it his land?' enquired my colleague, taking out his pipe, matches and tobacco pouch.

'It's everybody's. The path is used by umpteen of the villagers, and has been forever. Well, I will say Florrie dropped her bonnet along his footpath. I think it was near the iron gate. Like us, she was pedalling furiously and a breath of breeze sent it scuttling off. We were so anxious to get away from that horrid red-faced old man with his shotgun, our mob pressed on to the main road and her bonnet just got left behind in some ditch. Nobody's fault.'

'Indeed. Was it of some value?'

'Just a plain, ordinary straw bonnet, Mr Holmes. The sort we girls wear in summer.'

'Of course, pray continue.'

'Well, amazingly, the next morning Florrie's mother finds it on the porch step – the bonnet, I mean. Someone had returned it. Oh crikey, Mr Holmes, by the afternoon she was dead! Florrie died at ten past two. She passed away in her bedroom.'

'My dear young lady, you are still a trifle inexperienced so far as worldly matters are concerned. Alas, we shall all of us pass away at some time.'

'But the hat,' she cried. 'The hat, Mr Holmes, she became ill after putting on the bonnet! Did he curse it?'

'Now, calm down,' said I. 'You blame a straw hat for your friend's sudden fatal illness. Surely that's a trifle eccentric!'

'Oh Lord, I'm sorry Doctor Watson. I mean, can a man curse somebody, like witches?' she asked in a determined way. 'It's just all so peculiar how her face and feet swelled up. One day Florrie's a member of our cycle club, a crowd of us pedalling across the Downs, carefree and gay, the next she's passed away and to be buried in the churchyard.'

'Here in Pulborough?'

'Yes. Daft old Whitty the sexton's been busy preparing a grave for her. It's so unfair.'

'Well, anyhow, Doctor Watson and I are

delighted to meet you all,' exclaimed my companion. 'Would you care to introduce us, Miss–?'

'Oh, Tometi, Tometi Stevens. There are nine of us. Oops, I mean eight, now Florrie's gone. Amy, Jessi, Edie, Ems, Aggs, Prune, Dots and me.'

The young ladies smiled enthusiastically and nodded in our direction.

I observed some splendid bicycles amongst them – a Raleigh, Rovers and Townsend Coventry tourers. The ladies wore practical sporting clothing, blouses with leg-of-mutton sleeves and uniform long, chocolate-brown skirts and bonnets. But this collection of young ladies had not cycled to the church merely to look pretty and engaging.

'Florrie was murdered,' said the girl Ems, leaning her bike defiantly against the old sun-drenched stone walling. 'She *was*, Mr Holmes, we aren't sure exactly *how*, but she was murdered.'

'By that beastly old major.'

'Old duffer Carlton.'

'Well,' said our magistrate friend Phelps, pitching in. 'I'm not that keen on Major Carlton either, but I should draw the line at calling him a murderer. An old army man, certainly a landowner, but not a murderer. "An old duffer" is one thing, but you mustn't confuse the two. Your club was, in our official jargon, "trespassing", my dears. The footpath is the major's right of way. All right, no one cares and we all use it, but it's on his land. I mean, perhaps he threatened you with a shotgun but I doubt if he'd actually be prepared to use it.'

'You should have seen the major pointing his gun at us, chasing after us with that sniping, growling rat-catcher of a dog snapping at our heels,' said Tometi, flicking her flame-coloured hair and turning to leave.

That evening was spent quietly reading or catching up on case notes. How pleasant not to bear the heat and stuffiness of London. I believe it was one of the hottest Julys on record in the city and we were glad to be out of it for a fortnight or so. I was for an early bed and I went into my room leaving Holmes to potter about, extinguish the oil lamps, lock up. The clean country air down here suited healthy living wonderfully, and made one feel pleasantly tired after the day's exertions.

I thought of Tometi, such an energetic and persistent young girl. But murder was a very serious allegation and from long experience, watching Holmes deal with the very worst of villains, many of whom were regarded as perfectly respectable types, hanged on evidence provided by my colleague, I felt she had better watch her step in future. To accuse someone simply because you did not like them was not enough. Young people were always apt to be impetuous, anyhow.

'What on earth has happened?' said I, letting Tometi the redhead into our holiday flat the following morning. Ham and eggs were sizzling in the pan I had earlier placed upon the hob in our modest kitchenette, the greasy haze of frying bacon blending with wreaths of tobacco smoke coiling from Holmes's long pipe. He sat smoking contentedly in his dressing gown perusing *The Times,* a languid, droopy-lidded expression upon his features.

'Oh, it's nothing.' She smiled sweetly, placing a

brown paper bag overflowing with ripe and softened damsons upon the table, fresh from her garden.

'But your finger is swollen. Here, let me take a look. Bluey-black, Holmes, rather similar to a nasty wasp sting.'

'Poisonous – better lance it, Watson.'

'Yes, I'll stick this sewing needle over the gas to cauterise it. Tometi, are you allergic to insect bites or wasp stings? Hurry, think, Miss Stevens. Are you in pain?'

'Old duffer Canton's the only pain round here,' she answered mischievously.

'Do you feel faint, lethargic?'

'A little.'

'Not shivery?'

'No, Mr Holmes.' The girl hooted with laughter. 'All this fuss. Oh, it's in my bag, by the way.'

'What is, Miss Stevens?' asked Holmes, looking at her in his searching fashion.

'The bonnet.'

'Not that again. Really, your sheer gall and persistence impresses me.' Then his face suddenly darkened. 'Don't touch it,' said he, 'either of you. You handled that straw hat this morning presumably, Miss Stevens. But did not place it on your head.'

'No, why should I? I have my own hat. Oh, and I found out there are men who can curse, by the way. Cast spells. Warlocks, they're called. Is the major a warlock, I wonder? A fat old curmudgeon like that, I ask you!'

'Do stop prattling on about such nonsense, Tometi. Let me fix your finger. Here, I'll put some iodine on it and bandage it for you. You can stay for breakfast, if you like,' said I.

'Miss Stevens, you are certain you did not place the hat on your head when you perchance glanced in the hall mirror as young ladies are wont to do of a morning?'

'Pshaw! I told you, Mr Holmes, I put it straight in my cloth bag. Florrie's mother gave it to me as a little keepsake to remind me of my friend. Oh dear, I'm going to start crying again, sobbing my eyes out in a minute. They're burying her up at the church this morning, you know.'

Holmes had located a pair of tweezers and, leaning his tall, gangly frame over the kitchen table, plucked the straw bonnet by the brim and, always careful not to let it touch any part of his exposed skin, removed it from Tometi's bag.

'I imagine your finger swelled up when cycling over here on your Rover Tourer,' he commented.

'Mr Holmes, I wondered if perhaps I'd bruised it grabbing the handlebars when I got onto my bicycle before saying goodbye to Mama.'

'No, young lady, you pricked it.' My companion elaborated, 'Upon closer inspection of this damned clever hat, I extract from the crown a most singular barbed insect stinger belonging to a large hornet woven into the inner lining and held securely in place with a liberal dab of cow glue.'

'How disgusting!' shrieked Tometi accusingly, her pretty freckled face turning bright red. 'It's the major's doing – old duffer Carlton's to blame.'

'Miss Stevens,' said Holmes with a calm, detached air, 'you will excuse my presumption, but this poisonous hornet's stinger undoubtedly caused your friend's death. When Florrie put it on her head, placing her hands either side of the brim, the top of the hat pressing downwards upon her scalp would have caused a scratch, a tiny sting that would have barely registered. According to you, Miss Stevens, she became ill shortly afterwards. By Jove, Watson, this was no warlock's curse, rather a practical invention. A steady hand should have been required to affix the insect stinger so firmly.'

Suddenly the door burst open. It was our friend, the local magistrate, Rodney Phelps.

'Good morning, gentlemen. There are the remains of a fort on a mound west of the railway, possibly a catapulta used by a vigilant Roman garrison against the invader. Are you up for a hike and then lunch in the village?'

'Not at present,' said my companion seriously, whilst I shared out the fried rashers and eggs after reheating the pan.

'Ah, well, be seeing you both later, no doubt,' the impatient fellow replied before hurrying off.

After pouring us hot coffee I was relieved that despite her swollen finger, Miss Stevens was possessed of a healthy appetite and appeared very chirpy and bullish. She recounted many amusing tales concerning her club of young lady cyclists. However, at the end of our meal, refilling my briar pipe once I had taken my seat in the corner, I was determined that we should proceed with extreme sensitivity and caution.

'We must keep a steady ship on this,' said I, scratching away with a vesta. 'On no account, Tometi, are you to approach the major. Start throwing allegations willy-nilly at him and he could perfectly well take you to court, and that would not please your dear mother, I'm sure. Allow Mr Holmes to decide what steps to take. Don't do anything rash and act on your own impulse. Understood?'

She hurriedly ate a piece of crusty loaf and nodded.

'The major's seriously potty,' she managed to say between mouthfuls. 'An absolute stinker. I'm off to Florrie's funeral, anyhow.'

The funeral for Florrie Hepworth took place over at Pulborough Parish Church at 11 a.m. and was well attended. Most poignant was the number of safety and touring bicycles propped in a row against the churchyard wall.

At this early juncture neither Holmes nor I were entirely convinced Major Carlton was the guilty party. After all, the mislaid straw hat could quite easily have been snatched by someone else lurking near the footpath that day. It might be said that a person does not attain the rank of major by being a total buffoon. Having been an army man myself, part of the British regimental system, I rarely encountered a totally stupid high-ranking officer. I should disagree or become infuriated with their campaign strategy, certainly, but dismiss them as an 'old duffer', certainly not. Tometi had in her youthful exuberance perhaps severely underestimated him and his ability to go to law should her allegations be unfounded and he as a consequence slandered.

Further along the street we stopped off at the

village post office. My companion was anxious to despatch a telegram to his elder brother Mycroft, who, as a key consultant to Her Majesty's government, would have been privy to details of the major's army career before his retirement via Whitehall and a whole host of military bureaucracy.

At the time I was more concerned with purchasing a 2-ounce tin of my favourite Ships tobacco and I took my place in the queue.

'Damn and blast,' I heard a bluff old bespectacled chap say with an air of truculence. He sneezed and blew his purplish nose, which was both bulbous and veined, into his hanky. He wore a Norfolk jacket and knickerbockers in the style of a gamekeeper. I instantly took him to be an ex-army man.

'Lost me bloomin' wallet. Ah, here we are. Box of my usual coronas, Mrs Teal. Dashed hot weather we're having, eh?'

'Oh indeed, Major Carlton. They tells me in Lunnon the temperature's unbearable. My sister wrote to me from Ealing complaining the tarmacadam along her street was meltin' – meltin', I ask you. That'll be two shillin's and fourpence, major. Will you be attendin' the annual committee meeting over at the vicarage? Mr Phelps the magistrate tells me there is much to be discussed concerning boundary issues.'

'Yes, I've had a dashed lot of bother recently. D'you know, I was walking along my own footpath when I nearly got run down by that ruddy ladies' cycle club. A whole brigade of 'em – must have been doing ten miles an hour at least.

Forced me into the bloody ditch, nearly killed my dog. I had my huntin' gun under me arm so I pointed twin barrels at 'em and told 'em to clear off my land, what!!'

'Ha ha, I'd love to have seen their faces, major. We don't want none of them young cyclists runnin' us over, do we. Modern fad, so unladylike. What's the world comin' to. Never used to go on.'

'Good mornin', gentlemen, didn't see you there in the sunlight. Are you up here on holiday?' said the amenable old fellow, reaching out to shake my hand.

'Marylebone is scorching,' said I. 'It's the hottest July I can remember.'

'India's got nothing on this heat, old boy,' he admitted. 'And to think I served out there with my regiment for over twenty years. Dealing with the Dervishes, damned uprising an' all. Well, good day to you both. Cheerio, Mrs Teal.'

'Can you really in truth imagine that old chap, who must be seven and sixty at least, and by his beetroot complexion love his beef, port, brandy and cigars, having the latent ability to create a means of killing a young lady by tampering with her hat?' said I incredulously.

'I grant you, my dear Watson,' replied my companion, stepping out of the shade afforded by the post office shop into the unbearably bright, sweltering noonday heat, 'it seems highly improbable.'

We headed back to the blessed cool of our holiday let and flaked out. Slumped in the corner, sipping my glass of India pale ale, I was surprised to see our magistrate friend Rodney Phelps bound through the door not ten minutes after we arrived home. He entered our small kitchenette in a state of considerable excitement, waving a tiny package about.

'Major Carlton ... asked me to give you this,' he chuckled. 'When I told him the great detective Sherlock Holmes and his biographer Doctor Watson were holed up in Mrs Lawson's holiday flat, he could not believe it. He has read all of your adventures in *The Strand Magazine*. A slight, ah, problem, though. The girl Tometi cycled over to the manor last night and accused him of putting a curse on Florrie's straw hat, of being a confounded warlock. Furthermore, and I regret to say this, gentlemen, she really got his back up when she more than hinted that yourself and Doctor Watson here had been employed by the cycle club to bring him to summary justice and see that he hangs for murder.'

'Dear me,' said Holmes, charging up his clay, 'that's dropped us in very deep water. The major must have been most put out. Anyhow, what's that package you're holding?'

'Well, he asked me to give it to you. A present, I think. You know, it's a bit unfair, Tometi coming down on him like a ton of bricks. He was wounded out of the army and misses his chums terribly. Young people have absolutely no idea how much we owe the likes of him. I don't know what this generation's coming to. I mean, I can understand young fellows taking to bicycles but ladies – no, that's wrong. It goes against the female temperament. I mean, just look at that lot we've got tearing round Pulborough – nine of 'em all come whizzing along the High Street, nearly run you down and have the audacity to talk back to you as though you're a blessed moron.'

By now, Sherlock Holmes had ripped open the package. He held up the object to the light of the window.

'A meerschaum pipe. I'm more of a briar root man, myself. But I expect it'll smoke well enough.'

'I say, are you gentlemen up for a walk to the old Roman fort? I've been sketching all morning.'

'What, in this heat?' said I incredulously. 'Leave the catapulta site until later this evening, when it's cooler.'

'Very well, Doctor Watson. I shall call for you fellows at around seven. We shall take advantage of the local hostelry then.' Our friend departed, promising to buy us a pint of beer each at The Stag later.

'Put that pipe up on the window sill, will you Watson. I might try it later, although I'm not too keen on the meerschaum, myself.'

Later, the loud rap of the telegram boy disturbed me from my nap. He arrived bearing an official form. I straightaway handed the telegram over to Holmes, who was slouching over a newspaper, smoking a cigarette.

'An answer to your enquiry from Mycroft,' said I.

'Thank you, Watson. Pour us a stiff whisky, will you. Humph, dear, dear me. It appears Miss Stevens's intense suspicions concerning Major Carlton are highly justified.'

'How so?'

'Because, my dear fellow, Mycroft informs us

that the major was a bomb disposal officer, highly decorated, who won the George Medal!'

'I don't follow.'

'Surely a fellow who can defuse an explosive device, defeat its intricate mechanism, uncross delicate wires, penetrate the core of its diabolical engineering, is more than qualified to attach a poisoned hornet's stinger to the inside of a hat!'

'My God, Holmes, I can see what you're driving at. But he is an older fellow now.'

'The habits of a lifetime's career in the military are not so easily lost. My goodness, what's that horrid smell, Watson?'

The pipe I had earlier placed on the window sill was now smouldering, acrid grey fumes filling the kitchenette.

'It's a bomb, Watson. For heaven's sake, sling it out of the window.'

I leapt up, toppling over my chair, charged towards the open window and, grabbing the pipe, hurled it as far as it would go out into the garden. We heard a loud 'crump' as it exploded amongst Mrs Lawson's rose bushes.

We were both of us incensed, despairing, even, that anybody could have, through sheer spite, wished to inflict a severe facial injury over the simple action of striking a match and lighting one's pipe, that most manly and pleasurable of everyday activities with which we are all of us so familiar.

The pipe-bomb, a meerschaum with a curved amber stem, the bowl shaped in the face of the composer Franz Liszt, had been adapted to form an explosive device detonated using a heat source.

In this case, the summer sun had reflected off the window pane and intensified further as it shone through the cut glass of a crystal flower vase placed on the sill, creating a lens effect, causing the fuse in the pipe to ignite, the ensuing fumes warning us of the danger in time.

'It is he,' my companion exclaimed, disgusted at the low trick, jumping up with a passion before seizing his hat and cane and heading for the door. 'Something must have snapped with the major. Why should a highly decorated, brave army chap like that act so irrationally?'

'He should be publicly stripped of his medals.' I confess my temper got the better of me. 'Any-how, his manor is but a short distance from the parish church.' I took a further cautionary glance outside at the garden before we left. 'That rascal shall have some explaining to do.'

'Have you your service revolver handy, Wat-son?'

'I have it here, old man.'

'Capital. We are bound to inform the local coroner that an exhumation must be arranged post-haste. I'll wager the young lady from the cycle club was killed by that dratted hat, the hor-net's stinger immersed in some execrable veno-mous poison, a derivative of a deadly snake found in only certain provinces of India, no doubt. It is obvious Major Carlton now regards us as a real threat to his liberty. This murderous behaviour bears all the hallmarks of a basically "decent sort" gone badly off the rails. I propose a recurring fever brought on in the Tropics when on active service affected his reason.'

'Excusing his proclivity for murder just won't do,' said I. 'That blasted pipe could have disfigured you for life, Holmes. I'll see him hang.'

The major's property was an old-fashioned gabled house set in a large, evergreen-hedged garden on the outskirts of Pulborough village. From the church we took a brisk trudge up a path leading across some arable fields – the footpath where that unfortunate girl from the cycle club suffered the misfortune of mislaying her hat while out riding with Tometi and her friends. The girls had paid dearly for their breezy and innocent trespass, for out of an overriding sense of anger and outrage that he and his dog had nearly been shoved into a ditch and that the path on his own land was being used as a cycle route by a group of high-spirited, pretty young ladies, he saw fit to murder one of them. A ridiculously spiteful reaction, an action one could only attribute not to an aggrieved landowner, but surely a fevered madman!

I furiously tugged at the bell pull. Moments later an elderly housekeeper, a small, alert woman, hunched over and rubbing her hands, appeared at the door.

'Where is he?' My companion chafed with impatience. 'Kindly summon your master at once.'

'Are you gentlemen the physicians, perchance?' said she, arching her heavily tufted eyebrows in surprise. 'I've just sheeted him. And where's Doctor Crabbe?'

'The devil – I am a consulting detective, madam. We are here on an urgent matter concerning the gift of a "joke shop" meerschaum pipe and a filthy cold-blooded murder. Fetch the major, I wish to have words. It's deuced serious!'

'Too late,' the prim and proper creature replied with a frown, smacking her gums.

'I suppose he's made a run for it, eh?' said my colleague petulantly, tapping the tip of his cane upon the granite step, presuming the hunt for our fox might prove much more of a chase than expected.

'Lor' bless us, sir, Major Carlton won't be going nowhere. He passed on some twenty minutes ago,' she told us plainly. 'Sunk into his leather armchair with a deep sigh an' none of us have been able to raise him since. The old malaria to which he was prone may have had something to do with his death, according to cook. He just wasn't himself this last week or so.'

Hearing raised voices, a crowd of gossipy maids had gathered in the hall, their heads cocked at an insolent angle. Despite the housekeeper's protestations Holmes and I pushed past and lost no time carrying out a search of the lower ground floor. The major himself did not object to this unwarranted intrusion of his manor. He sat before the hearth, his corpulent frame sheeted like a ghost.

We found his study to be predominantly filled with angling clutter – nets, fishing rods, reels and tackle boxes – but there was a glass-lidded cabinet displaying pinned insects – butterflies, moths, wasps, bees and a variety of winged hornets.

The old oak desk, at which he had no doubt spent many hours conspiring and inventing, was festooned with an array of tiny, intricate instruments, a number of split-open 'No. 5' cartridge cases, cotton wadding, a powerful eye glass and, more damning still, the stale vapours left by a spirit lamp with a pot of boiled cow glue on top, the gum brush still stuck to the insides of a congealed mess of resin.

Later that afternoon we joined our friend Rodney Phelps, an avid student of prehistory, for a trudge up to the old catapulta site.

'Shame about old Carlton popping his clogs like that,' said he. 'A heart failure, the hot weather blamed. Not surprising; I believe this is the hottest July since records began in England. Do tell me what you think about this splendid hill fort, Holmes. The inhabitants dropped a large number of coins, many of which have been dug up.'

'A very notable ruin,' my colleague agreed, puffing on his pipe.

3

The Disappearance of Mr Hockley

One morning, having yet to wash and shave, I emerged from my bedroom and headed straight to the sitting room in search of breakfast, I was amazed to find Sherlock Holmes sitting with his chin upon his chest, his brow knitted, concentrating upon an item of footwear placed on a sheet of old newspaper.

Inspector Lestrade had taken the couch and

was smoking a cigar, pondering the greater meaning of this object.

'An old boot,' said I, laughing. 'Are we become a lost property office, Holmes? Do you want me to give it a good brush and polish?!'

My remarks on this occasion were not appreciated and I noticed the normally affable Scotland Yarder seemed to me dour and pensive, and considerably out of humour. Mister Sherlock Holmes himself was serious and contemplative to the extreme.

'Watson,' said he, puffing on his pipe and frowning, 'handle this boot with care. What are your initial observations?'

I sighed, snatching it and twirling it round by its laces.

'Hobnailed, steel toecap, leather uppers soiled and rather mouldy, greenish deposits I should identify as plant algae. Being submerged in filthy water for some time the boot is still in surprisingly good condition and passably wearable!'

'By Jove, you're on form, Watson. Pray, have you perhaps anything more succinct to offer? Take your time, by all means.'

'Good gracious!' I recoiled in horror. 'My God, Holmes, there's the remains of a human foot inside. Mostly skeletal but flaky particles of skin still adhere to the bones and leather inners. This really has become a nasty repository for a severed foot.'

'You know, Doctor Watson,' commented Lestrade, 'it's a grim old business. Imagine, if you will, poor Mr Creed toddling down the end of his garden one morning to clear his pond and finding this wrapped in weed!'

'The size is really quite distinctive,' said Holmes, puffing furiously on his pipe, a vaporous swirl of blue-tinged tobacco smoke curling up to the ceiling. 'Size thirteen or fourteen at least – a military style shoe, both sturdy and protective, of a kind worn by working men.'

'But how on earth does it end up in someone's garden pond?' I ejaculated. 'The foot was clean shorn off, Holmes, straight through the bone as if by a guillotine.'

'Precisely. I'll wager a considerable weight was applied, possessing a sharp edge.'

'I am reminded of an industrial accident of some kind – a fellow's limb entangled in factory machinery. But the matter of the pond still eludes me.'

'Mr Creed's terraced property is along by the railway?'

'Indeed, Mr Holmes, along the line operated by the Great Northern between Wood Green and Southgate. His garden backs onto the railway, separated by a tall wood-slatted fence,' said Lestrade, finishing his cigar and stubbing it out.

'Most promising. You know, I am convinced this army style boot belonged to a large, ungainly fellow. Perchance I am reminded of a newspaper article I consulted some time ago at the beginning of winter. Watson, would you be good enough to fetch that voluminous notebook from the shelf for me, month of October.'

Whilst I confess Mr Sherlock Holmes could on occasions be a notoriously lax and untidy individual, when working upon some fresh case my friend believed a clear and considered approach to be essential.

'My dear Watson,' he would say, 'for the successful process of deduction, one's brain attic must be on a par with a well set out library, a precisely sorted and catalogued index easily to hand, not a dusty heap of old boxes of books in disarray which we constantly stumble and crash into, unable to sift a single useful fact from the clutter, let alone recall urgent and relevant data when required.'

I rummaged amongst the row of bulky files and sheaves of papers until I came upon the aforementioned album of gummed press cuttings.

While I poured us both a cup of coffee from the pot I watched him keenly devour each hefty page, studying every article minutely.

'Ah, I have it!' said he at length, leaning forward in his fireside armchair. 'I shall read an extract from the *London Standard*. It says here: "Mr Hockley is a local man who started on the railway at fifteen, working as a booking boy in the signal boxes. He consequently worked his way through the grades until in his mid-forties he became a class 1 signalman, one of three employed at the east signal box. Upon the night of his disappearance he came on duty a minute or so before 6.00 p.m. of a Sunday, signed the register and was not due to sign off until early the following morning. However, at some stage during the night he went absent from his post and has not been seen or heard of since. A Mr Osborne, a relief signalman, was adamant that when he arrived to take charge, the small stove used to heat the control box was still warm, the kettle and teapot rested on the hob. A mug and pint jug of milk, a sugar bowl and a plate of bread and cheese were spread upon the table, the oil lamps trimmed and lit."

'A Great Northern spokesman was at a loss to explain the disappearance. Why the signalman should have abandoned his box, he did not know. The fog was terribly thick but luckily the line between Wood Green and Southgate was not busy that night. A footplate driver of the morning coal train was the first to realise something was amiss and reported the matter directly to King's Cross central office.'

'Could there have been a tragic accident on the line? Well, there were no signs of a body. Mr Hockley's mother described her son, a man of over six foot in height, as a "gentle giant" and was anxious as to his well-being.'

'I see your point about the shoe size,' said I. 'The coincidence is remarkable. What say you, Lestrade?'

'I recall the fellow was regarded as always punctual, industrious and never missed a day's work through sickness in his life. The east signal box was meticulously checked by us for clues to his disappearance, but none were ever forthcoming.'

'Well, the boot we have here with its skeletal foot intact suggests Mr Hockley is dead. The newspaper accounts for the time inform us no human remains were found on the track and the tunnel was searched, therefore we must deduce how one of his boots came to end up in a garden pond a good mile and a quarter from Wood Green signal box.'

'I have a theory,' said I.

'Bravo. What do you propose, dear boy?'

'Supposing Mr Hockley strayed on to the track

and got run down by a train. Might not a pack of roaming dogs or foxes have dispersed the human remains over a wide area? They are opportunists and scavengers, after all.'

'Hmm, a credible explanation, I grant you, but I should embrace a marginally less gruesome theory myself.'

'And that is, Mr Holmes?'

'That he was murdered and his body taken elsewhere.'

'The evidence?'

'You know, Watson, I am prepared to abandon our violin concerto at Wigmore Hall this afternoon to investigate this most singular of cases. A supply of the strongest shag and cigarettes is essential for our undertaking so we must visit Bradleys before embarking upon the Great Northern and venturing along the line to that part of London known as Wood Green.'

'To visit the notorious east signal box, and walk the length of the cutting?'

'To enquire at a public hostelry in the locality if anyone knew Mr Hockley. Perhaps someone can tell me a little of his life outside of the railway.'

'Well, I'm off to Scotland Yard to follow my own line of enquiry,' announced Lestrade. 'Let me know if you make any headway concerning the case, Mr Holmes. Meanwhile, I shall entrust you to take care of that old boot!'

'Very well, Lestrade. Come, Watson, we have a train to catch at King's Cross.'

The porter at Wood Green was quick to give directions. However, I felt far too indolent to partake of a half of India pale ale so decided to stay put and let Holmes get on with his discreet questioning. A sturdy bench and my briar pipe was all I required. I sat on the platform staring at the east signal box, a construction of timber and bricks situated to one side of the soot-encrusted, fume-filled tunnel mouth. How gloomy and claustrophobic it must have felt, manning the signal box in winter, the cutting shrouded in cold, clammy fog, marring visibility.

A number of passenger trains stopped in both directions before my friend made a welcome appearance in the ticket hall, looking very dapper in his silk top hat and well-tailored frock coat.

'By the spring in your step, I should say you have been successful in your endeavours at The Grapes public house,' said I, putting away my pipe and tobacco pouch.

'You are of course correct, my dear Watson. A Mr Jennings proved not only a first-rate publican but a most genial fellow possessed of a sharp and observant mind. He enriched my meagre knowledge of Mr Hockley's personal life considerably. I am now able, with some confidence, to identify the person who actually killed him.'

'Good grief, Holmes,' I exclaimed.

'Furthermore, I have a fair idea of the method. We are dealing with a double murder, by the way. Ah, I see our train is in. Watson, be a good fellow and keep a lookout for a patch of newly planted grass growing along the embankment. Keep your eyes peeled as we travel along towards Southgate. I am informed by a punter at The Grapes that our would-be murderer, a day or two prior to the signalman's disappearance, happened to purchase a spade and a sack of Bivingtons Easy Grow grass seed from the corner shop in Wood Green. Normally used to plant lawns and meadows, it will be distinctive from the longer and more untamed variety of grass growing wild alongside the track.'

'Grass seed? Have you lost your reason, old fellow?'

'On the contrary, my dear boy – we find ourselves upon the very brink of solving a most ingenious and well thought through horticultural crime.'

All the while our train rattled along, I could not help complaining. 'A double murder, you say Holmes, and here we are like a couple of ninnies surveying the embankment.'

'By Jove, pull the emergency chain, Watson. Stop the train at once!'

My friend leaned out of the compartment window and pointed frantically at a lush green rectangle of ground, distinctive from the rest.

'Grass shoots!' I exclaimed, stretching up and tugging the emergency cord for all I was worth, praying we should ourselves not be arrested for wasting railway time and causing an entire train schedule to be disrupted.

Thanks to the modern use of Bell telegraphs, Inspector Lestrade was soon on the scene. According to Holmes's directions, officers of police began prodding at the soil with long poles, testing the rigidity of the ground, whether chalky or clay.

I noticed the replanted grass was flourishing beneath the warm spring sunshine.

'Over here, gentlemen,' an officer called out. They had begun to dig in earnest.

'What do you make of it, Watson?' said Holmes, kneeling down beside a pile of recently excavated earth, examining what was obviously a body emerging from its earthy confinement.

'Dear me, old man, this is Hockley all right. The railway uniform is largely preserved, the dirty fabric clinging to human remains. See here, the official cap with its distinctive metal "GNR" badge. Oh Lord, and there's more. Under his decomposing body is another – a woman's – we can tell this by the winter skirt and feminine undergarments. It's a bally shame. Who is she, I wonder?'

'Mrs Baines,' said Holmes grimly, 'the wife of a train driver employed by the Great Northern.'

'You're certain, Mr Holmes?' asked the ratty-faced Scotland Yarder, scribbling away in his notebook.

'They were having an affair, you see, Mr Hockley and a married woman. He was openly affectionate to Mrs Baines in the snug of The Grapes. A foolish moment of intimacy was witnessed not only by the genial landlord Mr Jennings, but, alas, also by a punter who must have reported back to a furious and inconsolable husband that his wife was carrying on with another man. From that moment the love birds' fate was sealed. Oh, drat the female of the species and their romantic silly notions,' exclaimed the consulting detective under his breath.

'The well aerated acid soil has preserved the decayed uppers of a leather, steel toecapped boot,' said I. 'It matches the one found in Mr Creed's garden pond. Now we've got a left and a right foot!'

'Exactly so, it couldn't be plainer. And the method of murder, Mr Holmes, what do you deduce so far?' said Lestrade.

'Watson, Lestrade, is either of you perchance familiar with the ganger's trolley, a manually operated railway cart employing a long wooden handle to activate power by means of leverage?'

'Certainly,' I said. 'A single person using the rail trolley can attain a fair speed and travel along the line most effectively carrying tools, wood, or a quantity of gravel.'

'Indeed, Watson. It is both silent and free from steam boiler machinery, locomotion acquired by one person operating the handle. Upon the night of the signalman's disappearance, I propose that Baines lured Mr Hockley from his box by means of friendly banter before cold-heartedly garrotting the taller and stronger fellow at the base of the wooden gantry. The lack of blood, the thick fog and the nature of the cutting prevented anyone from witnessing the murder. I recall the local police were puzzled by a piece of dowelling found near the signal box – the length of stick perfect for garrotting the victim. A Spanish method of execution by strangulation – the knotted rope is attached and, once the rope is secured around the neck, twisted violently clockwise, tightening pressure on the larynx.'

'And the unfaithful wife?' asked Lestrade.

'Oh, he must have presumably killed her earlier, brought her to the railway and loaded her sheeted body onto the ganger's trolley. Then he manhandled the dead signalman on board as well, and headed off towards Southgate, a handy spade and a sack of grass seed accompanying him. At some stage the trolley jolted, perhaps on a join in the track – and Mr Hockley's body fell off, one of his feet becoming cut off by the edge of a running iron wheel.

'The rest is elementary. In a panic to reach the embankment, Baines simply replaced the body on the trolley and flung the boot, foot and all, over the nearest fence.'

Thus was concluded the case which appears in my notes under the reference: 'Railway Crime – The East Signal Box Murder'. It must be plain to the reader that by applying his elementary principles of practical reasoning Holmes correctly deduced that casual conversation with residents local to the area should prove of far more value than simply examining the vicinity of the cutting and signal box for clues which the police had already done with little effect – save for finding a length of dowelling which nobody could associate with any kind of crime until Holmes presented us with his astonishing revelation concerning the 'garrotting technique' used to fell a man well over six foot.

Thus, an observant publican and a punter chatting amiably to my companion over halves of India pale ale ensured a callous double murderer was brought to justice. But where were the bodies hidden? Somewhere beside the railway track would be the most convenient situation. The lush new patch of grass growing amongst all the older, wilder vegetation along the embankment gave the game away.

After the makeshift grave had been further excavated and certain nominal enquiries gone into by the police, Inspector Lestrade and a number of Scotland Yard men were sanctioned to make an official arrest and Joe Baines was taken into custody upon shunting his goods locomotive into buffers at the coaling shed at King's Cross.

As a footnote, that section of line upon the Great Northern became for a time a tourist trap after the story of the illicit love affair between Mr Hockley and Mrs Baines, with the consequent terrible double murder occupied front page headlines of the daily newspapers for a number of weeks, inflaming London's populace to a veritable frenzy of lurid curiosity.

4

The Giant Footprint

The Sussex Downs are of historic, as well as scenic, interest. On many of the higher points are the harrows, or graves, of British ancestors. Roughly 3 miles east of Crowborough and a little to the north is an estate, the owner of which has managed to implement an enterprising experiment.

Mr Hugh Waring became our nearest neighbour when we rented for a fortnight a white cob holiday cottage perched on the Downs some half a mile or so from the tiny hamlet of Shudbury-Staving.

Possessed of a fine Tudor mansion, which he had transformed into a comfortable farm house with luxury modern amenities, Waring additionally converted a nearby hunting lodge into a small private museum, of which, at a charge of one penny per head, he would show round visitors such as cyclists or ramblers who happened to stumble on that remote region in the summer. Therein was displayed his much coveted collection of fossils, cracked pottery shards, birds' skulls, unidentified fragments of calcified bone and a modest amount of Roman coin – in short, a fair to middling accumulation of finds a ten-year-old child should be proud of, but nothing in the least remarkable to the student of prehistory.

One afternoon, the weather being decidedly inclement, we decided to spend a dull half hour wandering around the polished display cabinets being lectured by our host. Waring's passion for amateur archaeology, his undoubted mania for collecting specimens, was in itself admirable. However, he seemed to consider nothing else in life worthwhile, save for collecting more and more fossils, else prising out of the agricultural landscape thereabouts old Roman coins of little value to the historian – pieces of bronze minted in their masses and owned by practically every schoolboy in England.

Anyway, if the discerning reader of this narrative has judged me a trifle harsh in my critique of Hugh Waring, fear not, for upon the third day of our holiday a momentous discovery changed everything – for a time, at least...

I recall after breakfast upon a sunny and blustery morning, we were smoking our pipes in the low-ceilinged sitting room, considering our plans for the day, when a loud and hysterical knocking at the door alerted us to our near neighbour's arrival.

'Mr Holmes, Doctor Watson, won't you come at once, gentlemen, I have made the most momentous archaeological discovery. The gods truly looked down favourably yesterday, for taking my customary walk I came upon an amazing find!'

'I'm afraid,' said I, 'we have only just finished breakfast, Mr Waring. We'll come across later, if you don't mind.'

'Cannot you spare a half hour or so, damn it?'

'Tell me, what have you bagged on this occasion?' Holmes responded caustically, wishing the fellow would leave. 'A crustacean fossil, a sparrow's skull?'

'I beg your pardon, Mr Holmes, a mere crustacean? I have discovered a rare footprint the like of which has not been gazed upon since prehistory. I'll expect both of you over at my house in half an hour. Better still, meet me where the main road to Lewes converges upon the road to Shudbury-Staving. Lunch will be served at noon.'

'Where that fingerpost is situated,' said I.

'Precisely, Doctor Watson.'

'Very well,' replied Holmes, stirring from his cottage chair to knock his pipe out in the hearth. 'We shall follow you presently. I trust our exertions shall not prove a wasted exercise.'

Grabbing our hats and coats we rode our

bicycles across the Downs. The weather was changeable and gusty and my tweed cap kept spinning off on a number of occasions, so that we had to stop and give chase.

I calculate we eventually arrived at the Lewes signpost at around a quarter past eleven. Further up the road, the undergrowth upon the verge had been recently beaten back with a stick. I recognised Hugh Waring's jacket hung on a branch casually.

'Over here!' I shouted, running along the road with my bicycle. 'Mr Waring, where are you?' I called out. There was no answer. When we reached the site I knew something was dreadfully amiss.

Face first in the vast imprint of some extraordinary gigantic beast lay Hugh Waring, the back of his head destroyed. It appeared, initially at least, that our neighbour had accidentally lost his footing. He was lying face down in a pool of blood, very still – very dead. One look at the back of his head was most disconcerting, for as a medical practitioner I was in no doubt he had suffered a fatal blow administered by some blunt instrument.

'What on earth's happened?' murmured my companion, taking out his pipe.

'Poor old Waring's had his head badly staved in.'

Barely had we a chance to assess the situation further and digest certain crucial forensic details, when a dog cart drew up. A red-faced bearded fellow wearing a straw boater with a narrow brim, collarless shirt, navy blue blazer and boating flannels stepped down and shook hands.

'Professor Sinclair. Are you chaps from London too? I've just travelled up from Kensington, the Natural History Museum, at Mr Waring's request. Luncheon is at noon, I believe. I'm expecting Johnny Atkins, who's an expert on *Hippopotami epidicopuli*, to arrive shortly. We're a gathering of historians and archaeologists, I take it, and no wonder! By Jove, he's not such a crackpot after all. This is a most rare and unusual footprint. But who's that lying down there?'

'The amateur archaeologist is dead,' said I with finality. 'We found Mr Waring like this not long before you arrived.'

'Can't be helped,' said he, unfolding a tape measure. 'Would you gentlemen be good enough to assist? I want to find out the width and depth of the print. I expect poor old Waring suffered a heart seizure. The excitement proved too much for him. The "discovery of the century" he called it, and he was right. Bit to the left, if you don't mind.'

'Are you an expert?' said I, astounded by the fellow's complete lack of respect, indifference, even, to Waring's corpse.

'I've travelled all round the globe looking for something like this. Antarctica, Africa, India – you name it.'

'The poor chap's dead,' said my companion bluntly. 'We can't simply ignore the body. He may have been murdered.'

'Murdered? Highly unlikely. No, let's honour his memory, he should have wanted us to carry on regardless. Once I've logged the site and our team has roped it off we can deal with the body then. This is much too important a find to be distracted with a death by natural causes. Ah, Johnny, glad to see you've arrived. Train journey down all right?'

A second historian, or expert on prehistory, was now on scene. He waddled along the grass verge to meet us. He was a tubby individual in white flannels, dabbing at his sweaty brow at every opportunity.

'Dreadfully slow, Professor Sinclair. Delay at East Croydon. My goodness, it was worth it, though. What have we uncovered here? A giant footprint preserved in chalk. *Hippopotami epidicopuli.*'

'No, Johnny. I'd personally plump for a hairy mammoth.'

'By gad, this is really very reminiscent of the Crockford Beast, a sort of giant hoof print we found near Woking in Surrey. Glad to meet you, gentlemen. Are you down from London too?'

'No, we are near neighbours of the deceased,' said Holmes, guiding that same gentleman closer to the edge of the excavation. 'We are on holiday. Mr Waring was keen to show us his find. Alas, he was dead when we got here.'

'Heart, I expect. Imagine – every enthusiastic amateur dreams of this sort of thing. Stumbling on something that will cause the map of Europe to be redrawn. Makes their name a household word around the globe. All too much for him, I expect. Simply conked out.'

'I agree, Johnny. The poor chap must have burst a blood vessel, heart given out. That, or tripped over and fallen in face first.'

'I must tell you,' said I, 'I am a doctor. The

injuries that are plain to see are wholly consistent with being hit from behind by a blunt instrument. Murder remains a distinct possibility!'

'Lunch,' said the professor emphatically. 'We can discuss this more sensibly over a bottle of claret and a good meal. The farm house is which way?'

'Through the hedgerow,' said I. 'There's a five-barred gate just up here. The path leads directly to the house.'

'Then let's all head for the manor,' Johnny Atkins proposed. 'We can contact the local constabulary from there. The sooner the body's removed, the better. My team will want to erect a tent and make a plaster cast of the footprint before evening sets in. The national press will have to be informed, of course.'

Over lunch that had been laid out already by his housekeeper, Mrs Tait, who was shocked to hear of her master's demise, questions were asked.

'Professor Sinclair, could you perhaps enlighten us as to the exact nature of this historic find?' asked Holmes, putting his plate aside. Hugh Waring's housekeeper had been tasked with contacting the local police force, a long and arduous procedure in this isolated part of the world. One of the servants had been dispatched to Lewes to alert the relevant authorities. Meanwhile, to argue as to the precise nature of Waring's death with these overbearing archaeologists, who seemed to have an answer for everything, seemed pointless.

'Well, gentlemen, the map of Britain began to assume its present form during the last geological epoch which roughly covers the period we call the Ice Age. A great part of England still lay under vast sheets of ice and glaciers. When the climate eventually warmed, Britain became a land of rich vegetation. All kinds of mammoth and rhinoceros roamed the southernmost parts of England.'

'Fascinating,' said I, finishing my pudding.

'My dear sirs, I have spent much time both here and abroad examining skeletal remains of mammoths. This enormous footprint our absent host came across quite by chance on his evening stroll bears an uncanny resemblance to either *Hippopotami epidicopuli*, known for its preference for swamps and tropical rainforest, or the hairy mammoth.'

'To the untrained eye,' said Holmes, striking a vesta to his pipe, 'it looks remarkably like a large elephant foot.'

'An escaped circus animal, you infer? Much too large for either Indian or African elephants, I'm afraid, Mr Holmes. Trust us, we know what we're talking about. Johnny and I have been studying prehistory for years. The Natural History Museum doesn't employ total asses. More wine, Doctor Watson?'

'Please,' said I, holding out my glass to be refilled.

We had not long finished lunch when the local constabulary arrived. An Inspector Finch, amenable but too easily overawed and impressed by the pair of archaeologists, headed the investigation. It did not take long for him to decide that death was accidental. A tragic heart failure from perhaps losing his balance or tripping over a stone. Waring, he wrongly surmised, had been overexcited by his magnificent find and, as a consequence, lacking a calm composure, became careless.

Holmes and I disagreed but we could do nothing. Every time we put forward our views, Professor Sinclair and the other expert from the Natural History Museum browbeat the police into their way of thinking, a mountain of opposition that Inspector Finch sided with. He agreed with their theory and we thus left them to it.

Anyhow, dare I say this: we were neither of us particularly fond of Hugh Waring. We therefore decided to return to our white cob cottage and continue with our holiday. But the case rankled and over our pipes and glasses of whisky we became more and more incensed, believing a miscarriage of justice had taken place.

'Of course he was murdered,' said Holmes, drawing the curtains to our cosy cottage, while I lit the lamps and settled down in my armchair. 'You don't fall into a ditch face first and mysteriously end up with a fractured skull caused by a blow to the back of the head. What a bunch of incompetents. That Inspector Finch was entirely taken in by the professor. Sinclair was his name, wasn't it?'

Holmes snatched a copy of the parish magazine from the small table and began thumbing through it, reading the parish notes and announcements of births and deaths avidly. 'Tara, tara,' he hummed to himself, the light fading and a flurry of rain no more than a summer shower pattering at the slate roof of our holiday cottage.

'Is there anything on tonight, Watson?' he remarked, placing the stem of his pipe in one corner of his mouth.

'I believe there is an amateur production of *The Pirates of Penzance* at Shudbury-Staving,' said I, refilling my briar. 'The village hall.'

'Good, good. We shall attend, Watson, and join in a raucous, riotous chorus of "When a felon's not engaged in his employment". Hello, what's this? A paragraph about Adams Acton, the famous sculptor – lives locally on the other side of the Downs towards Crowborough. Pedlars Dripping Pan – where the devil's that?'

'About a mile and a half's ride, by and large. Should reach there on our bicycles by half seven.'

'Upon my word, old chap. Let's get pedalling. It was murder, all right, but there's another interesting twist to this giant mammoth's foot business!'

Adams Acton was gaunt of feature with thick gremlin-like eyebrows and silver-grey bushy hair. His hands were covered in cuts and grazes ... the knuckles particularly so.

Holmes informed Adams Acton everything about the day's events. At first, the sculptor gave me the impression of being bemused ... bored, even, but, as the details unfolded, he suddenly slammed down his glass and told my companion to shut up!

'Now that's damn odd!' He wiped some droplets of whisky from his beard. 'I passed through Shudbury-Staving with my assistants, Jarvis and Ken, last Sunday on my way to Lewes. That's a bit of a coincidence, isn't it? Had an awful time of it, Mr Holmes. My old farm wagon leaned over several times – hub was loose on one of the wheels – but, if that wasn't bad enough, the cart for the job was too small and my giant granite sculpture tipped the damn thing over and fell off. Luckily we had a winch but it delayed our journey considerably!'

'A sculpture, you say?'

'Took months to carve! I should never have agreed to the project but my dear wife wants to extend the lily pond and put a Japanese bridge across it. Why are you looking at me like that, Dr Watson?'

'And what exactly was this sculpture?' I could barely conceal my amusement.

'Elephant's foot – solid granite – much larger than a real one, of course. Made it for a wealthy Parsee in India. It's going to sit on the steps of his palace. Mr Kangra gave me the commission when I was last in Bombay working on a statue of Major General Sir John Fenby, one time governor of the province. Ton and a half of jumbo's foot, I ask you! Hold it sacred or something, don't they? I suppose he'll want me to cast it in bronze for his living room next. Not one of my more classical, allegorical and heroic works.'

Back in London, a week after our Sussex vacation, when all the furore had died down concerning the discovery near Lewes of a supposed hairy mammoth's giant footprint, plus the hoo-ha surrounding the later discovery by Mr Sherlock Holmes that it was in fact nothing more than the dent left by a fallen block of masonry, neither of us was surprised to read in *The Times* obituaries that Professor Sinclair had blown his brains out.

To recount, Holmes, after searching the area

thoroughly, retrieved a typical archaeological trowel inscribed R.S. (Richard Sinclair) hastily concealed in a rabbit warren close to the main Lewes to Shudbury-Staving road. He quickly concluded that the professor of prehistory, wishing to claim all the credit and ensuing publicity for himself and Johnny Atkins, ruthlessly killed the amateur fossil hunter, Hugh Waring, not long before we arrived on our bicycles. He must have fled the scene after hearing our voices, and coolly returned in the dog cart, pretending he had only just come down from London, when in fact he had been biding his time, allowing us fifteen minutes or so before he turned up, shaking hands and full of archaeologist's bonhomie.

The fact that the hairy mammoth's giant foot proved to be the imprint of a large and notoriously heavy sculpture fallen off a cart, and that his reputation was in ruins, along with the guilt he bore for the callous murder of Hugh Waring, must have prompted Sinclair to end his life.

Holmes nonetheless assures me he would have pursued the archaeologist and eventually brought the professor to face justice, and thereby Hugh Waring's untimely death would have not gone unpunished.

5

The Discovery at Kew

I am not normally a particularly early riser and find it irksome to be disturbed from slumber, denied the simple pleasure of awaking by my own volition.

This was to be my lot when Inspector Lestrade took it upon himself to knock up our lady housekeeper at half past four in the morning, causing a volley of complaints to be directed at me and Mr Sherlock Holmes as we clattered down the staircase and made our way through the front door to the waiting cab. Wearing her nightdress, Mrs Hudson stood in the hall, sternly admonishing us, hair in disarray, lamp in hand, the unflattering shadows it cast making her appear like a veritable Medusa.

'Well,' said I, joining my companion and the Scotland Yard detective. 'That's going to take a week at least to clear the air! I cannot abide it when Mrs Hudson is displeased with us, Holmes. My nerves won't stand it. I should not like to be turfed out on the street with all my worldly possessions and forced to find other digs if you don't mind, Lestrade.'

Holmes appeared far from supportive, merely striking a match to his pipe, peering intently at the gloomy facades of the shops and double-fronted houses opposite, the yellow glimmer of the gas lamps reflected on the gleaming surface of the road.

'Now, now,' said our Scotland Yarder, buttoning up his coat. 'Women are such strangely mercurial creatures, Doctor Watson, who soon forget and forgive our little foibles. I'll warrant she'll be her old cheery self once you've returned from Kensington in need of a hearty breakfast.'

'Kensington?' I queried, searching in my coat pocket for my pipe and pouch of Arcadia mixture. 'Has a town house been burgled, then?'

'My dear fellow.' My companion puffed avidly on his briar-root pipe. 'Lestrade presents us with an intriguing problem – a first for the botanical gardens at Kew, I believe, inspector.'

'Indeed,' he replied in all seriousness. 'We are presently dealing with the recovery of a body, Doctor Watson, and a most queer place to find one, I must say.'

Some time later we were shepherded away from a large glass hothouse and conservatory, taking a pathway across the park towards the thickly wooded south-western section at Kew. Dawn was breaking over London and I confess I was at a complete loss as to the body's whereabouts until I observed a mass of crows squawking and bickering above the tree canopy. We joined a group of police officers, Kew officials and groundsmen who with glowing faces gazed purposefully heavenward at the sprawling branches of a tall oak tree growing amongst the horse chestnut, leafy silver birches and alder thereabouts.

A constable had climbed up the wide trunk and was securing a rope and pulley to what appeared to be a bamboo platform strung high up in the branches. At last, despite the attack of birds, he succeeded and a recovery of sorts took place.

'Bring it down gently,' the sergeant of police cried through a loudhailer. 'Patiently does it, Davies, don't make the damn thing wobble so. Tug more on the left rope, less on the right. Keep it level, for gawd's sake. How's the body bearing up?'

'Badly pecked, sir,' bellowed the other from a great height, accompanied by the sound of creaking, dripping branches. 'Darn big those rooks, too. I reckon every crow in London's wound up here at Kew.'

The makeshift platform, basically bamboo poles roped together, was lowered to the ground and at last we were able to gather round. A shrouded bundle lay secured to the top of the platform by means of dried palm fronds twisted and knotted together. The face of the deceased was concealed by an oriental decorative face mask much damaged by the incessant pecking of the crows. The shroud was pocked with tears and rips in the cloth, the material itself dirtied and smudged mossy green from having been up in the canopy for so long.

Holmes lost no time in examining the bamboo struts and the bindings with his magnifying lens before turning his attention to the reclining cadaver. Lestrade and I eagerly joined my colleague, kneeling beside him on the dewy, tussocky grass. We helped cut away the matted shroud.

'Hum, upon the thigh I observe clear evidence of

bite marks long healed, presumably from snakes, else poisonous insects. See upon the calves and ankles – scarring to the skin tissue caused by greedy leeches clinging on. By Jove, this fellow evidently spent much of his working life wading through rice paddy fields, or enduring long treks into the jungle; an explorer, perhaps? But I should favour our obvious links with Kew – a plant hunter, an experienced one, too. On removing the mask, the face appears too badly pecked to identify. Now, Watson, will you assist me in unfolding a little more of this sorry, tangled shroud to free his arm? Ah, we can safely detect from this deep indentation upon the third finger of his right hand the mark, of a wide signet ring. More light, if you please, inspector. See how the ring has been energetically prised off, else cut away with pliers. So in life the fellow wore this ring without hardly ever removing it. It was a deuced tight fit, hence the swollen knucklejoint. The inference of the tree burial is not entirely lost to me – the funerary rites practised by peoples from as diverse regions as India and Nepal to Bali and Lombok. The exact origin of the decorative mask escapes me.'

'Good gracious, sir,' exclaimed a gentleman wearing a bowler hat and tweeds, a florid-faced chap with mutton chop whiskers and piercing eyes. He drew closer with his storm lantern, his mouth hanging open in disbelief. 'You've practically described the man I know so well. This is my dear friend and fellow botanist, Cuthbert Glenny. The last I heard he was off to Bali in search of rare orchids. The Asprey ring was a gift from his sweetheart, Miss Violet Dunnwiddy, the daughter of the coal magnate Rawlings Dunnwiddy of Yorkshire. It was a token of her love and Cuthbert rarely took it off. They were to be married in Rudston. What a damn travesty.'

'Is there nothing remotely suspicious about this wretched business, then?' asked Lestrade, getting up and brushing himself down. 'No foul play suspected, Mr Holmes?'

'To summarise – by a process of natural decomposition and the consumption of the body by our busy London crow population it is difficult to determine whether the plant hunter was murdered or not.' My colleague lit a cigarette. 'Well, my dear Watson, there is nothing more we can do here. I suggest we return to our rooms at Baker Street and in more civilised surroundings enjoy a breakfast of rashers and egg. I am absolutely famished. Inspector, I shall wire Scotland Yard once I have had more time to consider the facts. Oh, and if you don't mind, I shall borrow this ferocious looking mask for a while. Good morning, Lestrade.'

Back at our digs in Baker Street, Holmes appeared locked into a process of repairing the grotesque mask to its former splendour. By gumming together the torn shreds of mashed, pulpy material and touching up here and there with water colours we were able to gaze upon the fierce visage of the object by the sunlight pouring in through the bay window.

'Interesting,' said I. 'No doubt it once belonged to an island race of cannibal warriors. The bulging eyes bore into you and the snarling mouth speaks of the cooking pot.' I folded over the page of my newspaper. 'I wonder if old Glenny met his end as part of a ritual slaughter, the plant hunter the victim of a primitive tribe of headsmen?'

'Here in London?' chuckled my companion. 'Really, my dear boy, that is a supposition taken too far. Yet I concede you may be correct to say that a ritual of some kind was involved.'

'I have seen similar masks at the Horniman Museum,' I remarked. 'From the islands of Penang, else Indonesia.'

'I prefer to conjecture it was once resident in Bali. What purpose it served, whether ceremonial or simply a decorative character in Balinese mythology, I have no idea. Anything of interest in *The Telegraph,* Watson? I've so far had little opportunity to peruse the morning editions. Where on earth is Mrs Hudson with that pot of coffee?'

'Our lady help is still fuming,' said I, browsing through the newspaper. 'I fear she shall cook us an inedible supper tonight and be slow to answer your summons. Lestrade knocking her up at half four has annoyed her. Ah, I see we have an afternoon of entertainment ahead of us at least.'

'Really, where's that, then?' asked my companion, putting away his gum brush and pot.

'It says here on page nine, "At two of the clock an exhibition of the Tuk Tuk Wan along with its golden portable ancestral spirit house at the Langham Hotel. For an afternoon only in the presence of the raja of Gianlong, the ruler of one of the oldest kingdoms in Bali." An event open to the general public and free of charge.'

'Whether the raja shall be able to escape Dutch colonial rule and a war is doubtful,' said Holmes.

'Political unrest means uncertain times lie ahead for him and his subjects.'

'Perhaps the raja could reveal more about this mask,' said I, lighting a cigar while my companion read the newspaper, taking in every detail of the article.

'The Tuk Tuk Wan is a compelling enough reason to venture forth to the Langham Hotel this afternoon, Watson.'

'Indeed.'

'According to this short paragraph, the Tuk Tuk Wan is one of the most precious and revered temple effigies in Bali, predating Hindu times. We are in for a visual treat, dear fellow.'

'And no entrance fee to pay, which suits my pocket agreeably,' I laughed.

'The Balinese treasure also provides us with a clear enough motive for why the plant hunter Cuthbert Glenny was murdered and left for the carrion crows to devour at Kew.'

At the Langham Hotel the foyer was crowded. A large room had been specially set aside for the exhibition of Balinese culture. After gazing upon various pottery, kites, basket-ware and bamboo furniture, we lined up in an orderly queue to pay our respects to the raja of Gianlong, who was hosting the event.

A completely westernised individual, handsome and dusky of feature, he wore the finest clothes Savile Row could offer, shoes by John Lobb, diamond tie clip, pocket watch and fob by Cartier. His noble fingers glittered with precious gems, and a sweetly perfumed garland had been hung round his neck by a liveried servant.

Although fluent in English he sometimes spoke briefly in Balinese. *'Roko-Roko'* he would say when requiring a cigarette. To me he was both charming and a gentleman of exquisite manners and breeding. He shook me warmly by the hand. My friend, meanwhile, managed to make the serene raja visibly flinch.

'The funerary rites of Bali interest me greatly, your Majesty. I wonder if you could explain how the experienced botanist and plant hunter Cuthbert Glenny ended up in a tree at Kew ... murdered?'

'Are you perchance the police?'

'I am a consulting detective and this is my companion, Doctor Watson. I am neither here to apportion blame or act on behalf of the official Metropolitan force, merely acutely interested to learn more about the plant hunter's death and the peculiar tree burial which I myself witnessed this morning at the botanical gardens in Kew.'

The raja, much to his credit, was both frank and to the point.

'Glenny was not all he appeared to be.'

'The Tuk Tuk Wan – he stole it, didn't he?'

'Indeed, from my principality in Bali. But listen, Mr Holmes, I cannot speak here. Await the unveiling and afterwards accompany my entourage up to my suite on the top floor. You have my assurance both of you will be made most welcome. I have nothing to hide and am certainly no common criminal capable of murder, as you infer.'

We had not long to wait for the unveiling. At a signal from the raja, a traditional silk cloth was drawn aside. For the first time the British public could gaze upon the notable golden effigy of the Tuk Tuk Wan. One could not help but be impressed by the bejewelled, ugly toad-like demon squatting on its haunches, a long spiky tongue dangling from its broad gash of a mouth, the writhing bodies of sacrificial natives being stamped beneath its enormous webbed claws.

'A guardian statue,' the raja commented wryly. 'A talisman of extraordinary power. A sacred effigy that for centuries was guarded by ferocious man-eating tigers prowling the temple grounds beyond the walls of my palace. But fear not, my dear British guests; although ugly as sin, he is but a rice field toad. Oh, he is so very, very lucky and I am sure he will bestow good fortune on you all.'

For our audience with the raja of Gianlong we were ushered into a small anteroom, being naturally denied access to his personal apartments where his queen and other wives resided privately.

'Dear me, where to start.' He shrugged, offering us each an Egyptian cigarette while his valet poured tea. 'Cuthbert was a ripping good fellow, absolutely charming and a wonderful and most attentive guest when he stayed with us at Puri Gianlong. I still retain his gifts, intricate drawings of rare plants and orchids, a personal notebook of his travels in Asia Minor, a number of photographs. Such a nice, companionable fellow. I trusted him, you see. We were both educated at Eton and Cambridge and I am myself an amateur botanist. We were of roughly the same age and outlook, the obvious difference being I am blessed with wealth beyond avarice and am ruler of a kingdom with a responsibility to my subjects, many of whom incidentally would gladly sacrifice themselves for me should the need arise. I was thrilled when Glenny first wrote to my secretary explaining that he would be visiting Bali in search of rare orchids and would I perhaps like to accompany him on field trips to the temples of Bedulu and Makam Jayaprana.'

'Forgive me, your Majesty, but to cut to the chase, am I right in thinking Glenny was not only a plant hunter but a tenacious hunter of precious artefacts which he hoped to sell for financial gain?'

'How profoundly perceptive of you, Mr Holmes. I'll be generous; maybe he was hard up, needed money to bolster his forthcoming marriage or on a childish whim he decided to double-cross me and steal the effigy. It matters not. What does matter is that I am at heart a botanist, a gardener, a lover of nature, you see. I felt so damn betrayed. My consort, Queen Bhumi, will tell you I am "an obsessive" and spend much time improving, re-planting, nurturing flowers – reinventing, if you will, the paradise I inherited from my father. My life, however, is not without problems. I have the Dutch to contend with and political tensions run high. I may yet have to raise an army to stave off the European aggressor. The problem with Cuthbert Glenny was that he crossed a line and stepped into dangerous waters from which even I could not save him. Listen, gentlemen, despite ruling an old principality I am myself a modern man well aware of all the latest telegraphic devices, the ebb and flow of the financial markets in London and New York, and so are my closest advisors, my inner court. My dear father insisted both his future heir and those closest to him should be up to date with all the latest developments in the industrial world. Glenny's huge mistake was to gaze upon my ancient palace and the temple grounds, pass through our villages with their shrines and bamboo huts and regard our culture as quaintly primitive – conveniently backward, if you prefer.'

'And pray, when did you learn of the Tuk Tuk Wan's disappearance, your Majesty?'

'Over lunch. Cuthbert was supposedly gone to Karangasam in search of rare plants. One of the monks came to me and told me the ancestral spirit house, the portable golden casket, had been simply unlocked, the temple effigy removed, the key replaced on its hook. I knew who the culprit was, of course.'

'No palace guards, no security,' said I incredulously.

'Up till now there was no need,' the raja answered tersely. 'Such is the mysterious hold of the Tuk Tuk Wan over my subjects that none should dare gaze upon it without permission, let alone steal it. We are not normally a race of people who go around in a state of suspicion at every turn. Neither are we stupid.'

'So, from that very moment you learnt of the robbery his fate was sealed.'

'I had no choice, I was forced to act quickly and decisively. A magnificent deception was required. Both my advisors and I were certain Glenny was headed for England. After all, his marriage to Miss Violet Dunnwiddy was not far into the future. It was imperative we got there ahead of him, firstly to reclaim the Tuk Tuk Wan, secondly to punish the perpetrator of this heinous crime. A meeting of our council was convened, a number of proposals put forward. It was decided to form a delegation and visit London. We informed the British government by wire that our intention was wholly peaceful and that we should like to launch an exhibition of Balinese culture free of charge to the public, to which your Foreign Office readily agreed.

'By now we had learnt the plant hunter was aboard a slow-moving cargo steam packet bound for Southampton. It would take ages to reach port. By dusk my delegation and I were on board one of the fastest ocean-going liners in existence. For a vast, unprecedented sum I had caused a White Star Line vessel to be diverted in mid ocean to rendezvous at Lombok. Now we were set fair for England; a swift and luxurious voyage ensued.

'However, that same night, Queen Bhutu asleep beside me in my berth, I dreamt of the golden Tuk Tuk Wan. The revolting toad seemed to be alive, smiling benignly as blood gushed from its broad mouth and poured down its enormous tongue. It was stamping its feet excitedly.

'I awoke sweating, feeling profoundly apprehensive, but of course my consort assured me that all was well, for since the last century at least, despite its ugliness, the demonic toad has in our land become synonymous with good luck, so I learnt not to worry and trust our enterprise should prove successful, which it was.'

'So at Southampton your people were able to

intercept Glenny?' asked Holmes, lighting another cigarette.

'Outside the customs shed. He was carrying a large, cumbersome carpet bag, the silly, stupid fool. A carpet bag, I ask you!'

'How was he killed – strangled? Stabbed?'

'I do not care how he was killed, Mr Holmes, and neither should you, Doctor Watson. It's done, he was basically a crook. The temple elders afforded him the greatest dignity. Monks performed the rites of a tree burial at Kew, his body nobly raised to the skies to be devoured by carrion crows, his spirit set free from the cycle of birth and rebirth. They took into account that part of his life which had been fruitful and studious, his interest in fauna, his love of wild orchids. If only he had not become greedy for gold, betraying my trust, the outcome would have been very different.'

6

Death of a Client

Selly Colnbrook was for many years the acknowledged doyen of critics amongst Fleet Street journalists representing theatre, literature and the arts. It was said his cruel nib was capable of sending a West End play crashing down in flames, else causing the latest swish novel, promoted widely as a potential bestseller, to become quickly ignored by the public and un-sellable.

He was loved little and hated beyond measure by the majority of publishers, authors and playwrights, yet despite his formidable reputation for negative criticism he could on rare occasions be praising in his judgement and offer meagre encouragement to the lucky few. Whichever view you took, most crucially he was one of the most popular and well-read journalists of his generation. Readers of both the *Evening Chronicle* and *The Telegraph* lapped up his weekly reviews of books, plays and the arts and he was noted for his wit and cutting sarcasm.

Therefore, it was with some interest that Holmes and I learnt in the obituary columns of his sudden death after a short illness, and barely a week had gone by when his lifelong agent and good friend Oscar Wheelan chose to call upon my esteemed colleague at Baker Street to air a number of concerns which had been troubling him.

I recall it was the middle of November and the season of fogs. Sherlock Holmes lounged indolently upon the sofa clad in his dressing gown, staring listlessly at the gloomy murk, smoking his long pipe.

'Well, my dear Watson, upon this crepuscular November morning, I may be forgiven for quoting Goethe, from *The Sorrows of Young Werther:* "Unhappy man, are you not a fool? Aren't you deceiving yourself, what avails this raging, endless passion?" Ah, is that footsteps upon the stair? A visitor may yet assuage our boredom.'

There was a loud knock at the door. Oscar Wheelan entered our rooms, a short, stocky individual of barely 5 feet in height. He had something of the pugilist about him. He was a top flight agent with plush offices in Shaftesbury Avenue, who during a long and successful career made a substantial sum of money for both himself and his elite roster of clients, for he was rightly regarded as a ferocious and stubborn negotiator of contracts. We knew of him due to his long association with the popular actor and theatre producer Charles Lemon whom we dined with occasionally at Simpson's-in-the-Strand.

'Well, Holmes, Doctor Watson, what a damnably foggy day. The traffic is choked so I decided to hoof it from Portman Square and walk to Marylebone.'

'Such admirable exertions, Oscar, deserve a cup of strong coffee. There's plenty in the pot. Come closer to the fire and draw up a chair. I read of the passing of one of your clients, Selly Colnbrook, in *The Times* obituary. His scathing reviews shall be sorely missed, no doubt.'

'What a card, what a character! But you know, Selly was a miserable, pent up sort of fellow who seldom attended literary lunches or first night parties. He wrote those mostly controversial reviews for the papers and that's all you got. He spread himself thinly. His last review was for *What Katy Did,* a play at the Haymarket.'

'But you look drawn and anxious, Oscar. Is something the matter?'

'Mr Holmes, I should be grateful if you could cast a preliminary gaze over this hastily scribbled note I received shortly before his death. On the face of it you might say it was damn funny, but now I'm worried I may have ignored a sincere plea for help.'

My companion rose from the sofa and snatched the epistle.

Dear Oscar
Dog called – box of Belgian chocolates in its mouth – canine delivery. Is it a joke – a new innovation by Fortnum & Mason? Since I ate the top layer am feeling damn unwell. Mrs Parsons scolded me for my esurience, sent me straight to bed with a hot toddy. Have a fearful chest cold coming on, much catarrh. Difficult to walk anywhere without running out of puff.
Regards,
Selly

'You fear that your client may have been poisoned, I take it?'

'Exactly,' answered the agent decisively.

'Watson, do you perchance recall that time you caught up with me at the chemistry laboratory at the University of London, not the first occasion with your old dresser, Stanford, but later when I was clearing out those sample bottles of alkaloid and pharmaceutical poisons – all manner of toxicity from antimony to strychnine. A passing student, a Scotch fellow, McBride, mentioned *powdered radium,* which neither of us had ever encountered before, and I'd totally forgotten about it until now.'

'Very difficult to isolate and identify,' I conceded. 'I've since read in a medical journal that radium presents all the natural symptoms of a common cold followed by the onset of pneumonia. It is more widely available in Russia where there have been certain notable poisoning cases attributed to it.'

'Why do you prefer powdered radium?' asked the agent, snipping off the tip of his cigar. 'Isn't *arsenic* the British way?'

'Because it would be perfectly easy to add to chocolate confection. You would not be required to dissolve, liquefy or inject it.'

'That's damnably smart. Poor old Colnbrook wouldn't have stood a chance. Why, he possessed such a sweet tooth and would have polished off half a box in one sitting!'

'How long was it between the note being delivered and his death?'

'Three days. Of course, he was in hospital with pneumonia by then.'

'No doubt died of a bronchial attack,' I surmised.

'Oscar, have you any idea as to the brand of chocolates? Were they Bourneville? Fry's, I wonder?'

'Well, it so happened I travelled by train to Brookwood Cemetery for the funeral from Westminster Bridge Road and on the journey met a fellow mourner, a Mrs Parsons, who for longer than I can remember was his daily help. Cooked his meals, swept the stairs and kept the rooms tidy at his house in Cloak Lane. After he died she told me she cleared out a whole lot of rubbish for the dust cart and remembered throwing away an empty chocolate box. The brand was exclusive to Konstantin's, the bespoke chocolatier who supply Harrods and Fortnum & Mason. It's a small shop tucked away in EC4, established by Russian émigrés – two elderly sisters, Irma and Polina Petrovich.'

'By Jove, you have done your work convincingly, Oscar. I've half a mind to recruit you for this little enterprise. Watson, be a good fellow and pour us all a whisky and soda. Afterwards we must venture forth into the foggy metropolis in search of Selly Colnbrook's nemesis.'

'I am at a loss,' confided the agent, puffing on his cigar. 'Where to start?'

'On the assumption we are correct in thinking the doyen of critics was poisoned and that foul play is suspected, it makes perfect sense, therefore, that whoever wished him dead was a person who had at some stage been deeply offended, bankrupted, even. Langton Lovell, the theatre manager at the Wimborne in Drury Lane, assured me simply enormous sums of money are sunk into productions in the West End these days. I should wager a resentful playwright, a novelist bearing the bitterest grudge, else a producer who invested much capital and lost heavily are all on our list!'

'You are correct, Mr Holmes. Selly was a popular but poisonous critic of the arts. His trademark cutting sarcasm and witty asides proved wonderfully popular with readers of the *Evening Chronicle* and *The Telegraph,* but he must have made enemies, there must have been those who suffered under his ruthless pen.'

The agent wiped his smooth pink brow with a handkerchief, remembering a long list of casualties who had written to him over the years complaining bitterly that Colnbrook's acerbic reviews were totally heartless and undeserving. Some tearful playwrights and authors, many of them poor and despondent about the future, even managed to turn up at his office to remonstrate, and how many of those had emerged from lowly garrets and tenements with barely a crust to live on between them?

'I concur,' said Holmes brightly, sipping on his whisky and soda. 'If needs be, Oscar, we shall consult every one of his negative, damning newspaper reviews for the last year, for I am certain therein lies our answer. For now I should very much like to visit our exclusive chocolatier, Konstantin's, so let us proceed to EC4. On such a sulphurous, foggy morning as this a cab should be too slow and dangerous. The underground railway is our best option, I think.'

The chocolatier Konstantin's we found to be a tiny, hidden away shop with a thickly paned bow window near St Stevens Walbrook in EC4.

The door bell clanged. We entered the premises, stooping before a low timbered ceiling.

'Good day to you both.'

Holmes walked briskly across to the counter, where two black-skirted old ladies sat smoking their hand-rolled cigarettes.

'Welcome, gentlemen. We suffer another London winter but I tell you frankly, in St Petersburg the cold and snow are almost unendurable. Please, take your time. The chocolates, I take it, are for your wives or mistresses. An ounce of assorted chocolates in a ribboned box gladdens a woman's heart immeasurably; a half ounce of delicious truffles smoothes the marital path, creates for the refined lady a bliss of pure indulgence. What month are we in now? Ah yes, November, and the fog lies so thick us pedestrians are forced to travel the dingy streets in fear of our lives with torches of flaming pitch. Polina, show our customers around.'

One of the old women was about to get up but Holmes insisted she stay put.

'Please, madam, do not leave your chair on our account. I observe you smoke a coarse tobacco favoured by the Estonian peasant.'

'A lifetime's habit,' answered the younger of the sisters. 'We are addicted to the filthiest cheap tobacco – Machorka. It has been our weakness since childhood when we would find such sweepings or dregs of cigarette cartons placed in a wooden box by a kind-hearted shopkeeper for us poor. Would you care for some?'

'Indeed,' said my companion, filling up his pipe and relishing a smoke of the obnoxious weed. 'You are both of you Russians, I take it?'

'My name is Irma and this is my sister, Polina Petrovich. You too have something of the restless émigré about you.'

'I am, it so happens, of French ancestry. My, is that a dog I hear barking?' Holmes removed the pipe from his mouth and listened.

'Only Oleg the husky. He wants his meat and bone meal. Do not concern yourself. Have you chosen yet, gentlemen?' she rasped, coughing repeatedly. 'The Tsar and Tsarina be praised. The longer we sisters live here in London the greater is our longing for mother Russia. Bah, that is the lot of us émigrés.'

'An acquaintance tells me Konstantin's chocolates are brought in by Harrods of Knightsbridge.'

'It all began from this little shop in the City and we do modestly well, don't we Polina? But still we must work and toil all the hours God sends us to survive. That will be two shillin's, gentlemen.'

A till register rattled and pinged as money and goods were exchanged. Our various purchases wrapped and paid for, we hastened out of the shop Konstantin's and made our way to the underground at Cannon Street. As we took the escalator to the lower level Holmes was jubilant.

'Watson, those Russian ladies Irma and Polina own a dog, do they not – Oleg?'

'Unusually, a husky.'

'The breed is one of the most keenly intelligent and obedient animals known to man, after it is tamed and trained, of course. Touchingly their eyes look almost human, quite disconcerting at close quarters,' said he, taking my arm and walking along briskly, the agent Oscar Wheelan trailing behind. 'Though more adapted to hauling sledges across snowy wastes than settling down in front of the homely hearth with its master.'

'A muscular guard dog.'

'They can be aggressive, certainly. I have read somewhere that they will eat each other when hungry and show no quarter to even their own kin,' Holmes remarked.

At Marcini's we were fortunate enough to share a table with the actor Charles Lemon and his business manager, Langton Lovell, both of whom were theatre impresarios who had kept the Wimborne open to packed houses, putting on many productions over the years. The patron of the Wimborne was the prominent reformer Lord Asprey, and Holmes had solved a pressing case for him in the past. We ate a delicious meal and afterwards, over brandy and cigars, chatted amiably.

'William Gladstone is the best prime minister we've ever had,' said Lovell, leaning heavily in his chair. 'You know he insists on visiting the East End and counselling fallen young ladies. It is his wish that prostitution be wiped out altogether, but of course the forces of the night are way too strong. The crux is he wishes to reform gently, to re-educate these poor women, offer them a better choice in life.'

'Economics dictate otherwise,' said Charles Lemon dismally. 'Just visit the Haymarket or stroll along the Thames Tunnel of a Saturday evening. The trade these street ladies turn over is astonishing. If you're of the fairer sex and poor and starving, moral values, however fine and upstanding, do not put bread on your table, else clothe your children. But I agree with you, Lovell, Gladstone has his heart in the right place. And what are you up to, Holmes?'

'Perhaps you could help put a fresh slant on the matter at hand, Charles. You must be aware that the doyen of Fleet Street critics is dead. Selly Colnbrook is no more.'

'Yes, I believe he was buried at Brookwood Necropolis. Look here, old man, I shouldn't speak ill of the dead and I know Oscar was his long-term agent and everything, but I absolutely hated him. Shall we let the matter drop?'

'Love him or loathe him, murder is a serious issue.'

'Murder? You mean you actually care? Leave be, Holmes, the man's just not worth it. The amount of pain and resentment credited to his wretched review pages should act as a counter. He was a pariah, too fond of his own bigoted opinions, prepared to sink a play just out of keeping his readership amused. You won't find me or Lovell shedding tears, I can tell you. The lights on Broadway and the West End won't be dimmed to honour his memory either.'

'I'm clutching at straws, Charles. Does a Russian actor or producer come to mind when the name Colnbrook is mentioned?'

'The out of work actor Katkov, noted for his Bohemianism, once told me an author living in his tenement block committed suicide over a stinging review in the *Evening Chronicle*. They were part of a sort of commune in Clerkenwell, a haven for Russian literati living in London, if you will. You might try there for a useful lead. A great actor, Katkov, a shame I cannot offer him a part in our forthcoming production of the divine and ever popular Anton Chekhov's *Uncle Vanya*.'

By late afternoon we found ourselves in Clerkenwell, traipsing along the foggy Farringdon Road. Poverty and overcrowding were the lot of this down-at-heel neighbourhood, lonely garrets within tall rows of tenement houses a refuge for certain poor and destitute poets and authors living by their wits, hawking a coffee-stained, ripped and worn manuscript, yet barely able to afford postage to send it on its way to a prospective publishing house.

We had enquired at a corner cafe as to the whereabouts of one known to us only as Katkov and the proprietor told us that the gentleman, a 'resting' actor, shared lodgings with a sick and ailing waiter by the name of Pyotr Veslóvsky. He gave us directions and a quarter of an hour later we approached a set of steps leading to No. 73. The front door was ajar so we ascended a flight of stairs to the next floor where a hive of tenants could be found working away in tiny rooms, staring despondently at silent typewriters, else poring over blank sheets of paper, awaiting inspiration.

Outside one of these cramped boxes I could hear the whistling of congested lung-sacks, the tired sighs of some poor exhausted invalid, fighting for precious breath before breaking out into fits of coughing.

'He should be hospitalised,' I whispered to Holmes. 'He is a long-time sufferer of pulmonary tuberculosis.'

There in the gloom of that curtained rat warren, my companion leaned over the bedclothes and gently shook the young man's bony shoulder.

'Katkov,' said he, pausing to allow a further fit of raucous coughing to subside.

'My room mate is presently out on business. Could I be of help?' The poor fellow, with a sallow face and longish moustache and brilliantined hair parted to one side, struggled to sit up, a handkerchief stained by blotches of blood clenched in his fist.

‘A trivial matter. Lie back and rest, Pyotr. My friends and I merely wish to ascertain how the “doyen of critics”, Selly Colnbrook, met his end. I wondered if any actor, author or poet amongst you could shed some light on a minor discrepancy of pathology. You see, we have taken a large and substantial bet among ourselves as to whether he was poisoned or not.’

The invalid broke into a fit of giggling, the already strained bellows of his weak and congested lungs wheezing and whistling an accompaniment. After a little time he composed himself sufficiently to continue.

‘Oh, him. He was, I am told, poisoned, murdered by a strapping fellow newly graduated as a doctor from Kiev University in Russia who perchance stayed briefly in our community before moving on to the City. I will tell you all I know, most of it gleaned in conversation with dearest Katkov.

‘On the next floor above ours lodged a sweet-hearted, dreamy pipe smoker by the name of Ivan Yulyevich, a young novelist originally from Kiev, who was lucky enough to be accepted by a London publisher. His manuscript, which he gave me to read, was a sharp, commercial piece of work titled *Winter’s Snowmelt at Gaspra,* the story of a gay young hussar and his love, set in the Crimea. He pulled out all the stops, an unashamedly fast-paced romantic fiction which I quite liked.

‘Next, I am horrified to learn tenant Ivan Yulyevich, resident of Clerkenwell, threw himself under the wheels of an omnibus in Hoxton and was taken to hospital, where he later died. You gentlemen must realise what caused him to take his own life. A filthy, low review dripping with malice penned by Selly Colnbrook, which appeared in both *The Telegraph* and the *Evening Chronicle,* dismissing the novel as rubbish. As the critic himself put it, 'A wearisome repugnant plot, dear discerning reader, book best avoided.' His vitriolic review was enough to destroy any reputation the author might have enjoyed. Seriously, he took his own life because of it.'

'Regrettable,' murmured the agent Oscar Wheelan, biting his lower lip, desperate to leave the writers' hovel, to quit the sick room in case he became infected. 'Very regrettable.'

'Indeed. Well, one morning I hear Ivan's brother's turned up, a fellow who's just graduated from Kiev University, and he and Katkov got acquainted. Not long after, he apparently, quite by chance, saw a room advertised above a chocolatier Konstantin's in EC4. According to Katkov he was befriended by two old Russian ladies who fussed over him and cooked his meals. The women owned a pet husky called Oleg, and I am informed that Ivan's brother and the dog bonded and became inseparable. He would feed Oleg his meat and take the dog for walks regularly. I know little else of the details. Fair to say, though, that Oleg became over time a willing accomplice and one evening delivered to the house of the critic in Cloak Lane a box of the bitterest dark chocolates.'

Outside the tenement, I was surprised to find Holmes feverishly agitated, a look of concern prominent upon his wan, hawk-like features.

'My dear fellow,' said I, 'I feel somewhat deflated. There is nothing left to solve, the matter of Oscar's old client cleared up sufficiently for us to return to Baker Street.'

'Not so,' said he gravely, drawing us both beneath the meagre light afforded by a streetlamp and showing us a piece of paper. 'A threat to the prime minister – oh the poisoning case is done with, but this ... this, Watson represents a serious threat to our own dear democracy. Gladstone's life may be in danger. Oscar, have you the time?'

'Half past six of the clock,' he answered, snapping shut his gold repeater before, like me, examining the hastily written note beneath the gas lamp. It read thus:

Katkov,
Together we shall see the end of a prime minister. Meet me outside the Whitechapel bell foundry at eight o'clock.
Yours,
Alexis

'I purloined this scribbled note from Pyotr Veslóvsky's bedside cabinet. By Jove, Watson, this Katkov is a queer egg all right.'

'It presents a considerable challenge,' put in Oscar Wheelan doubtfully. 'How on earth are we to hire a cab and cross London in time, Holmes? The fog is dismally thick, we only have a couple of hours at most.'

'Yes, we shall have to head Shoreditch way. I conjecture Gladstone shall be out and about doing charitable work amongst the poor and needy of Whitechapel, ministering to the fallen women. The Russians Katkov and Alexis intend to strike him at his most vulnerable. Hurry, summon a cab, Watson.'

Our cabby proved indispensable for he knew the most direct route and did not lack courage either, for our four-wheeler was soon rattling along at a cracking pace following Old Street through Shoreditch, Hackney and Bethnal Green until at the bottom of Cambridge Road we entered the precincts of Whitechapel, the horses trotting along until our four-wheeler pulled up outside a short terrace of Georgian houses on the corner of Fieldgate Street.

Loitering in the damp fog, we saw two burly fellows with a little lamp greet each other outside the bell foundry before hurrying away. I am afraid to relate we managed to lose them in a network of narrow cobbled alleyways, but later along by Toynbee Hall came a rousing cheer, a commotion as a crowd of street women, clothed in rags, surged forward, hustling each other to get a better view of the frock-coated prime minister taking time out from government to address the epidemic of prostitution.

Thank God we had reached him before anything amiss occurred. Followed by the crowds, striding along the street, the grand old man of British politics waved benevolently.

Thereafter removing his top hat, Gladstone, the classical orator and veteran of political speeches, ducked into a slum of a terraced house and through the grimy window it was possible to see him being led to a chair. The crush to get inside was great, the overpowering stench of squalor pitiable, but Holmes nonetheless pushed forwards and we managed to find a space.

I felt every sympathy for the fallen women of Whitechapel, but then something incongruous occurred that shocked my sense of decency.

The common herd parted and a lady of disrepute had the gall to approach the prime minister and coquettishly sit on his knee, grabbing him round the neck, smothering him lavishly in wet kisses, which the old fellow did nothing to discourage.

The street women roared and clapped their approval, but to us this represented amazing effrontery, a serious breach of etiquette. A gentleman does not openly degrade himself in this fashion, but there was far worse to follow. While the two embraced, a camera flash exploded, causing spots to dance before my eyes. A photographer was strategically placed near the door with his box camera and tripod.

'That's not the sort of behaviour I expect from a British prime minister,' exclaimed Oscar Wheelan, totally enraged and at a loss as to what to make of the debacle. 'And where are the policemen and his aides who normally accompany him?'

'An impostor,' cried Holmes, snatching up his loaded hunting crop. 'A damned dirty impostor. Watson, be a good fellow and smash the glass negative plates. Hurry, it's Alexis who is the camera operator.'

'Leave him to me,' said I, taking up my stout ash stick and advancing through the melee of stinking bodies, fully intent on smashing the photographic equipment and destroying it good and proper. Oscar was at my side, ready to help restrain Alexis the camera operator. The Russian saw us coming but we were quickly upon him.

Holmes, meanwhile, seized the supposed prime minister of Britain and Ireland, tearing off his grey-haired wig and stuck-on mutton chop whiskers. The convincing disguise was demolished in a jiffy, the putty nose and heavy jowls forcefully removed. A humiliated Katkov was seized by the scruff of his neck, marched out into the street and, along with Alexis, tied up to a wrought-iron gas lamp, one of the row lining the pavement.

'You devil,' he seethed. 'I had not been able to find work for months, the West End and provincial theatres closed to me. I am a fine actor, sir, who revels in costume drama.'

'You were a damn convincing Gladstone, Katkov. You are a scoundrel of the first order and had us all fooled. You perfected his walk to a tee and the theatrical grease was applied flawlessly, but you can't simply impersonate the prime minister in order to take compromising, morally decadent pictures. You were playing the blackmail game, Katkov, and dealt your ace, but were trumped fair and square by me and Doctor Watson. It's a lengthy stretch in Botany Bay for you, I'll wager, and your compatriot Alexis.'

7

The Sea Funeral

Wreathed in a fug of pipe smoke that had settled in a haze before the mantelpiece, Holmes glanced up from behind his newspaper and was moved to say, 'That old seadog, Rear Admiral Sir Hugh Montmorency, is to be cremated at Golders Green Crematorium at noon, Watson, followed by a burial at sea of the urn of ashes off Newhaven. The obituary is well enough written, anyhow. The memorial service is to take place at St Paul's next week. We have been invited to attend today's funeral service at Golders Green by the admiral's solicitor, Mr Eaves.'

It was a chilly spring morning towards the end of March, the breakfast things tidied away and our familiar bachelors' routine progressing to our mutual liking. I was endeavouring to clean the stem of my old briar pipe with spirit of meths. 'Yes, he was a first-rate commander,' I acknowledged. 'Sailed an armoured gun boat up the Yangtze River and quelled an uprising in Shanong Province. A Chinese opium overlord was beheaded. The prime minister shall sorely miss his sound advice on naval matters. The admiral clearly never forgot your kindnesses to him when clearing up that ugly blackmail business with the young cockney upstart.'

Footfalls on the stairs caused Holmes to crumple his newspaper into a ball and sling it across the room.

'A Herr Volk to see you, Mr Holmes.' Our landlady, Mrs Hudson, popped her head round the door and announced our visitor.

'Magnus Volk of the experimental seaside railway? By Jove, it can't be the same fellow!'

'It is, sir,' said our visitor, entering our sanctum. 'I have come down from Brighton by the train and took a hansom from the terminus to Baker Street. I am honoured to meet you, Mr Holmes, and this, I take it, is your acclaimed biographer.' He shook Holmes's hand warmly. The little man in his drab, black suit removed his bowler whilst my colleague indicated the sofa and refilled his long pipe from the Persian slipper beside the mantelpiece.

'Tobacco? Cigar?'

'I prefer cheroots, thank you Mr Holmes, although if I may trouble you for a match.'

Once our visitor was comfortably settled, Herr Volk presented a wholly perplexed and careworn individual.

'You are a pioneer of electricity,' said Holmes, tamping down the dottles of last night's smoke into his pipe bowl. 'I suppose you must be here on a related quest. Are your numerous patents under threat, an infringement of copyrights?'

'Not exactly, though you are close. The matter I have come to see you about does indeed concern one of my electrical inventions, though it is classified as top secret and you will be unfamiliar with the *synchrocyclotron-arachnid*, more commonly listed by the military as "The Spider", due to it having four pairs of independently operable mechanical legs.'

'An electricity machine,' said I. 'So you've come up with a newfangled armament, I take it.'

'Heaven forbid, Doctor Watson, I should never dream of inventing a device for slaughtering people. It is entirely against my principles, and that of my wife and family. Nay, mine is an invention of mercy, a mechanical Florence Nightingale, if you will.'

'I am intrigued,' remarked Holmes, striking a match to his pipe, stretching his long legs in front of the hearth, 'though I confess this *synchrocyclotron-arachnid* sounds as sinister as it gets. Pray, does it benignly dispense medicine on a ward?'

While I chuckled at my companion's witty aside, Herr Volk blew out a stream of smoke from his cheroot, proceeding to offer us an explanation of his secret device.

"The Spider", gentlemen, is purely an aide for the recovery of wounded or dead soldiers on the battlefield by means of pneumatic pincers, lessening the risk to stretcher bearers when under fire. Only last month I tested a prototype along the beach, demonstrating to the Ministry that the bolted parts are both watertight and able to withstand wet, boggy conditions. The power supply comes from a long cable fed to the monitoring cabin, a converted reinforced steel bathing machine, and with practice a child could operate it. The levers are simplicity itself.'

'Forgive me interrupting, Volk, but presumably one of the reasons you find yourself requiring my services is that such a supposedly benign machine could be potentially altered in times of war, say by some foreign power, to use against us as a mobile weapon of destruction, an unmanned machine gun, for example.'

'Precisely. You understand my predicament, and why I shall be going straight to Whitehall from here, for two nights ago the plans for the iron arachnid were stolen from my garden workshop, the locked and secure filing cabinet in which I normally store my drawings and calculations expertly picked. The thief knew what he was after, for The Spider's plans were the only documents stolen. Listen, gentlemen, I am a civilian inventor; my little railway runs beside the beach at Brighton from the aquarium to Black Rock daily, a seaside amusement beloved by children and grandparents. I have no wish to become the latest Armstrong, stocking all his immense wealth from guns and ammunition. The *synchrocyclotron-arachnid* was designed to assist the Red Cross and the Royal Army Medical Corps to retrieve wounded servicemen under fire. Now I find myself facing a government investigation, with Whitehall terrified that the plans for this electricity machine will fall into foreign hands. Me, me, me, it's all centred on me this morning, and I absolutely detest the intrusion into my working life. But what's a chap to do?'

'Herr Volk,' ejaculated Holmes, springing up from his fireside chair and pacing up and down. 'You have my assurance that Doctor Watson and I shall do everything in our power to retrieve the plans. Your journey from Brighton was not wasted. However, I must ask you to be patient.

The armament industry is building up apace in Germany. Will you return, say, tomorrow night? I may have something for you then. I agree with you, Volk, it's a dratted bore having to deal with Whitehall bureaucracy. Watson, how long until the admiral's service?'

'We have a full two hours before it commences,' said I, handing Herr Volk his bowler and accompanying him downstairs to the street.

For his service at Golders Green Crematorium, the rear admiral (ret.), who for his latter years had resided in Hampstead Village, was blessed with fine, sunny weather. There was still a nip to the air, but it was exactly what he would have wanted for his send-off. Mourners were a mixed bunch of convivial friends, relatives and naval top brass. The service was to be a gay affair, no maudlin faces or weeping tolerated, a burst of Gilbert and Sullivan by an amateur players' association, a witty ship's chaplain, 'Flighty Cavendish', steering proceedings and a rousing sea shanty to end. As the curtains swished discreetly across the plinth on which rested the admiral's coffin and the remains were lowered by means of a hydraulic lift to the furnace room beneath, the odd clank and whir of pulleys accompanying its brief descent, I realised I had seldom enjoyed a funeral service better. However, while we waited in our pew for a crowd of people to pass, Holmes was aware of a troubling discrepancy.

'That's queer, Watson.'

'What is, old man?'

'You observe the gas wall heaters.'

'Yes, there's a double row of them.'

'Not to labour a point, but on every previous occasion I have attended a service at Golders Green, for instance the funeral of Alf Cropper the safe-breaker, else Sir Edward Creighton the top civil servant, the mantles of the wall heaters flared up after the curtains swished across.'

'Oh, why's that, then?'

'The gas flow in the crematorium building, including the chapel, is regulated from the furnace room beneath us. As they prepare to slide in the coffin it swells in the pipes. I am no physicist but to incinerate a body properly the ovens must be heated up to a fearful temperature, hence the increased gas flow precipitates a sudden flaring of the mantles upstairs in the chapel.'

'Remarkable. What should we deduce from that?' I asked, gathering my hat and stout ash stick, preparing to leave.

'The crematorium staff downstairs are delaying burning the coffin for some reason, perhaps unscrewing the lid to look inside.'

'But that's surely against the rules, Holmes. The staff must guard against shoddy working practices. Why, not long ago there was a blessed scandal at a south London crematorium. The removal of the deceased's jewellery – rings, tie clips, pocket watches, bracelets – without the next of kin's permission, and sold for profit.'

'Yes, I recall reading in the *Daily Chronicle* the miscreants were arrested and later charged.'

Outside the doors to the red brick chapel we mingled with other mourners and, there being a short delay before the commencement of the next funeral, allowed ourselves to pause on the steps and reflect upon the old admiral's long life and career.

'I suppose they'll box up the ash,' said I at length.

'Urn – urn, if you please, Doctor Watson. After all, we are not intending to give Sir Hugh a pauper's funeral,' laughed old Mister Eaves, the admiral's executor, of Lincoln's Inn. He patted Holmes's shoulder fondly.

'My client was always grateful to you for clearing up that dispute with the young man. We are about to return to the admiral's Hampstead home for drinks and a choice of buffet. There's plenty of room in my landau, gentlemen. I should be honoured if you would accompany me back to the village. After the buffet lunch we catch the train from Victoria to the port of Newhaven where we mourners shall again liaise with the funeral directors for the final journey out to sea in the tugboat *Alborada*. A sea burial is planned for sunset.'

'Most appropriate. I shall be with you directly, Mr Eaves. I am just going to make enquiries at the crematorium office.'

'Bless my soul, what's got into the fellow?' said the puzzled solicitor, shaking his head. 'The crematorium office? What does he want there?'

I decided to keep my own counsel but imagined the flaring gas mantles had something to do with my friend rushing off like this. Was there some illegal racket going on here at the crematorium, I wondered?

A sea funeral was something of a novelty to me. I

had never attended one before and was interested as to the order of procedure. We arrived on the boat train from Victoria to the port of Newhaven and were ushered off the platform and taken beyond the warehouse sheds to the quayside where granite stairs led steeply down to the deck of a squat, powerful steam tugboat. *Alborada* was berthed along by the harbour wall, her stout hull immersed in gently lapping, oily green, murky water.

We waited whilst a couple of undertakers carrying the urn descended the steep steps first. Amongst our crowd I recognised Teddy Alderton, the First Sea Lord, Sir Clive Hood, a long-time resident of Hampstead and a close friend of the deceased, and John and Lucy Montmorency. A number of ratings joined us, a piper amongst them, and we filed down the steps, preparing for a voyage out to sea. The smelly engines of the tugboat clattered away and smoke billowed from its funnel as we clambered on board and shifted aft.

The raucous shouts of seamen uncoiling ropes and setting lines free signalled our departure and *Alborada* was soon chugging up the harbour past colliers and tall sailing ships, barges and flotillas of smaller craft towards the breakwater built out from Barrow Head.

'Well, Holmes,' said I, 'have you anything to report on your impromptu visit to the crematorium office? Were the admiral's rows of medals or his gold pocket watch stolen back at Golders Green? Are the staff on the make?'

'A far more serious issue presses upon us, dear boy. I learnt from a lady in the office, Mrs Marks, that a new member of staff, a fellow of Germanic extraction, Heinz Gerbier, was recently recruited by the council offices in Hendon, and also another crematorium assistant called Werther.'

'Germans. Is not an Englishman up to the job? Are we a race of slovenly loafers all of a sudden?' said I, incensed.

'That said, tell me what you make of that undertaker, the stiff, formal fellow with the face set like a block of marble. He holds on to that urn of ashes so fervently, like his life depended on it, which incidentally it probably does.'

'He is typical of their type,' I remarked. 'Dour, pale, a falsified sense of gloomy introspection about him.'

'I refer to his footwear, old fellow.'

'Good heavens, Holmes. He wears a pair of worn-out hobnail boots. I'd expect better, fine polished Chelsea heels or square-toed patent leathers!'

'Press on. Now regard his clothing. You will notice, I am sure, the frayed ends of a boiler suit poking from his finely creased black trouser bottoms. Move up and we find a sooty, grubby, unwashed neck. Evidently he makes a slovenly toilet and prefers a working man's outfit to winter long johns beneath his everyday wear.'

Despite Holmes's reservations, I can report the sea funeral passed without incident. The admiral's ashes were sprinkled into the choppy English Channel just as he would have wished. To the sound of the pipes of a naval rating, the sun set fair over East Sussex.

However, upon our return to port I have seldom

seen Holmes so restless and fired up. With a steely determination he hurried me along the windy breakwater to a public telescope available for holiday tourists. 'Have you a penny for the slot, dear boy? Perchance we can peer through this fairly strong lens out to sea. There is still light enough.'

'The horizon is dimming,' said I.

'Just so – ah, I knew it!' he exclaimed. 'I knew our stony-faced undertaker was up to something rotten. That's it, crowd round. Tell me, what do you see, Watson, bobbing up and down on the ocean swell?'

'A tiny marker buoy with a flag that glows in the dark, coated with phosphor,' said I sombrely.

'Not a buoy, but an urn, my dear fellow. I think it prudent that Herr Volk of Brighton be contacted straight away. I must send off a wire for we have imminent need of his expertise.'

'Volk? But why does the urn float so well? What keeps it anchored?'

'Ah, once retrieved I am certain it shall have the signature of Heinrich von Schimmel, alias Werther, writ large all over it. Only he could turn an urn into a marker buoy and have the cleverness to conceive of such an intricate mechanism. Cork-lined, Watson; a clockwork timer no doubt triggers the flag to flick up on a hinged arm, the timer resets and a plumb line conveniently drops through flaps in the base, sinking to the Channel bottom, thus securing the urn and making it seaworthy. The Germans must have been waiting for the opportunity of a sea funeral, biding their time, making sure every last detail was perfected. Golders Green Crematorium has much to answer for.'

By late evening Herr Volk had joined us, his steel reinforced bathing machine in place upon the shingle beach beneath the steep chalk cliffs. I, like Holmes, was astounded when the *synchro-cyclotron-arachnid* was unloaded off a wagon, an enlarged metal spider with innovative electric headlamps for eyes.

'It is perfectly stable in water,' said he, making a check of the underside. 'And by a mere turn of a brass knob in the control cabin it becomes a submersible, able to manoeuvre underwater as well as on land. The lengthy cable is our force of contact.'

'Volk, will you send your beloved creation across to that marker buoy, the cork urn. Can you sink the iron arachnid roughly beneath?'

'We can try our best. I shall myself control the machinery, Mr Holmes, but I must emphasise it is a prototype.'

Later that night, while Holmes and I surveyed the calm, moonlit sea with binoculars, a sailing vessel was seen approaching the coast, the finest streamlined racing yacht I ever saw. It anchored further out but from the deck was launched a small rowing tub and this, under the stewardship of a burly oarsman, made slow but steady progress towards the bobbing urn.

'Are they the Germans who were employed by the council offices at Hendon to work as crematorium assistants?' said I.

'Exactly so, Watson. It was their intention to be prepared, for months, if necessary, for the opportunity of a sea funeral to arise. The rear admiral's death reported in the *Hampstead Echo* and more popular broadsheets should have alerted them to the possibility at last of stealing the top secret plans for Herr Volk's innovative *synchrocyclotron-arachnid* and pressing into action a secure means of smuggling them out of England onto the Continent. The Germans, of course, neglected the possibility that I should be among the list of mourners invited to the service at Golders Green, a foolish error for which they shall pay proportionately.'

The rowing boat was soon bearing down upon the glowing marker flag and the buoyant urn snatched out of the water.

Holmes signalled the control cabin with his dark lantern and not long after a bubbly cauldron of frothing foam and lashing sea spray heralded the emergence of the iron arachnid. Under the glare of its two menacing headlamp eyes the boat was instantly capsized, one of the men killed as it smashed to matchwood. However, the other unfortunate fellow, still clinging onto the urn, was dragged by mechanical pincers back to the shore. I feared that his bones might be broken, else his arms wrenched from their sockets, but Volk had designed this machine in such a way it behaved gently, thus our German spy was recovered further along the beach, spitting water, cursing, but otherwise unharmed.

'Welcome to the south coast, Herr Heinrich von Schimmel, I trust you found our English Channel to your liking? Although the water, I have heard, is a bit chilly at this time of year. By the by, Fernly and Bredon from the War Ministry will be glad that the plans have been safely recovered. They shall be here shortly. Prise open that urn, will you

Watson, there's a good fellow.'

Waving a lamp about, Herr Volk came stumbling down the beach from his control booth, elated that one of the spies had been captured, yet concerned that the iron arachnid, by means of seawater entering the complicated array of fuses encased behind the headlamps, had short-circuited. The whole machine now lay heaped uselessly beside a slanting groyne. The acrid smell from overheated copper coils hung heavily in the air, the narrow furrows etched by its legs in the shingle evidence of its awkward, grating journey up the beach.

'Well, nothing a spanner won't fix,' remarked the inventor, knowing full well it would take a massive amount of time and effort to overhaul his prototype.

'Your spider proved a most efficient and adroit workhorse,' said I, but then I froze, for three gentlemen were approaching us with raised guns gripped in their hands, mean and ruthless by the look of them.

'Hold up your hands or we'll shoot. All of you.'

Volk, who had barely wriggled under the battery housing to access repairs, must have supposed the crunching footsteps belonged to the civil servants Fernly and Bredon, for he had hardly bothered to glance up.

Holmes stared frostily at our hostile beachcombers, his stern unbowed expression never relenting.

'The plans, gentlemen,' the taller individual with thickset Teutonic features and wildly untamed springy hair said politely. 'Give them to me.' A thin smile crept across his lips. 'A pity those two

Whitehall civil servants are tied up on the wharf. What incorrigible ninnies you Britishers are! Pass me the plans or you all die. Can it be simpler? Can it be plainer?'

'Very well,' answered Holmes, reluctantly passing him a much-creased envelope marked 'Top Secret'. 'You German fellows are smart, damned smart. I failed to guess you would naturally possess back-up. I am heartily depressed, but there we are.'

'Your cooperation allows me to bestow the gift of life. Hermann, Geisler – untie Heinrich and let's scram. You look wet through, von Schimmel!'

The Germans hurried off along the beach heading towards the dockside, their shadowy figures soon lost to the blackness.

I admit I consequently felt rather glum, the bravado knocked out of me. I sighed heavily and was about to pass comment when a hand familiar to me rested gently on my shoulder. I heard both Herr Volk and Sherlock Holmes burst into peals of boisterous laughter.

'Look, old man,' I implored, 'this is not the time for hysterics!' I must have sounded irritated but I hated losing my wits like that. 'Pull yourselves together.'

'My dear Watson, our laughter is in celebration, not girlish histrionics!' said he kindly. 'The contents of that creased envelope marked "Top Secret" were only a folded bit of old newspaper. The plans for the *synchrocyclotron-arachnid* are safe, deposited in Herr Volk's zipper wallet. After you prised open the urn I gave them to him for safe keeping. I believe it is prudent that we get out of here rather quickly before they realise their mistake.'

A couple of days later, the heart of the great city was drenched with bright spring sunshine, the weather shaking off the last of the long winter, the parks lush and verdant, trees budding into leaf. Holmes and I decided to take in an afternoon concert of Beethoven and thus found ourselves forming part of an orderly queue along Kensington Gore, home to that fine glass-domed auditorium, the Royal Albert Hall, a building well appreciated for its unique acoustics. The concert was to be played by the Berlin Symphony Orchestra under the baton of von Strumm, a conductor widely feted in Germany but little known here.

The balcony seats overlooking the concert platform were ideal to watch the orchestra warming up. I nudged my companion, for I had noticed something odd.

'Holmes, that principal cellist looks very much like Hermann, one of the gunmen who accosted us on the beach at Newhaven.'

'That's deuced peculiar, Watson,' said he tentatively. 'You know, the leader of the string section is absurdly reminiscent of Geisler, the other gunman. Is the world renowned Berlin Symphony Orchestra become a nest of spies, I wonder?'

But it was when the conductor walked out onto the rostrum and the audience at the Royal Albert Hall politely applauded that we understood a spy ring was indeed endemic in the orchestra, for von Strumm, with his wild untamed hair, was none other than the ruthless agent who had demanded Holmes hand over the secret papers and threatened to shoot us.

8

The Kidnap at Novodevichiy Cemetery

The year 1898 saw Holmes and me travelling abroad to Russia on diplomatic business. The Foreign Secretary had entrusted my colleague with a confidential letter, a proposal of strategic military and economic advantage to both our nations addressed to his counterpart at the Kremlin.

This mission accomplished, taking into account that the whole of Europe was snowed under and travel restricted, it was decided we should delay our departure and take a short stay at the Hotel Metropole near Teatralnaya Square. Having slept comfortably the first night I recall a dull, grey January morning, a cold, swirling fog rolling off the Moskva River and snow lying thickly packed and crisp upon the Moscow streets when a little after ten we received a visitor from Peredelkino.

I confess that neither I nor my companion, Mr Sherlock Holmes, have ever had cause to venture south-west of Moscow into the forested countryside, but I am informed that there are situated in this wooded region many dachas belonging to wealthy persons of rank and influence, of decided culture and refinement, among these the affluent banker Perevin of the Grand Financial. It was our great pleasure that morning to invite into our suite of rooms his youngest daughter, Raisa, a coltish, fair-haired girl, high-spirited, pretty and vivacious who, after allowing me to help remove her huge fluffy white stole and beaver fur hat, took a chair before the decorated fireplace and began to explain at a childishly breathless pace the reason she had desired an interview so fervently.

'"I saw her, I saw her. It's her!"' I gasped, pointing a finger at a photograph on the front page of *The Moscow Times*. '"The girl who was kidnapped at Novodevichiy Cemetery."'

'"Lida Bezlukov, the daughter of the Iron King,"' Olga, my sister, exclaimed, holding me close to her, "the oligarch who owns all the iron works and grinding mills around Moscow and northern Russia and is worth a fortune. Raisa, Raisa, why are you so perplexed? It's not like she is one of our relatives or a friend of ours. Half a million in ransom demand – the old goat had better pay up, or else!"'

'"I saw her when it was dark," I replied, '"in a street near the Konservatoriya. It is her, Lida Bezlukov, or at least – oh, dear me, maybe it's not exactly her. I mean to say, what if she's already been killed by her captors? What if she's not like us any more, Olga?"'

'"A ghost."' My sister guffawed, her eyes watering with merriment. '"Don't be so perfectly ridiculous, Raisa, you'll have me dying from mirth. Here, allow me to dry my eyes. Next you'll be asking Papa for one of those mystic Egyptian planchettes and alphabet cards. We can discount your silly ghost as a doppelganger. Talk sense if you can, darling Raisa. I mean, either you saw the real Iron King's daughter, her twin or a lookalike. Which is it to be, dearest sister?"'

'"A phantasm,"' I answered emphatically, storming out of the room in tears, our familiar old servant the plump and jolly Sophia in tow, desperate to make me happy again.'

'Wise counsel from your sister Olga, I think, Miss Perevin. The recent kidnapping of an oligarch's daughter is the talk of all Moscow. I am beholden to the general manager's secretary, Mme Kalita, for informing me of the latest developments. Well, well, half a million by the middle of the week. The ransom must be paid or she'll end up in the river, apparently. Do you smoke, by the way?'

'I will have a cigarette, if you please. The case is sensational. A beautiful girl kidnapped from a cemetery, whisked away to God knows where. Is Lida Bezlukov still alive or is she dead? The police can only guess how it was done! Why, Mr Holmes, it is fortunate you are in Russia. The official force in charge of the investigation seems, from what Muscovites read in the newspaper, to be floundering around in the dark.'

'You are most kind, Miss Perevin. Over breakfast in the dining restaurant Doctor Watson and I were most interested to hear mention of that larger-than-life-size statue erected in Novodevichiy Cemetery purportedly cast out of solid gold, at a cost of God knows how much, which surmounts the tomb that will one day house Lida Bezlukov's father, the Iron King of Russia himself.'

'Journalists' say-so, rumours, an entire fabrication, tittle-tattle spread by the press. Goodness, what an absurdity to sell newspapers. It is in fact cast in bronze, Mr Holmes, cast in his own image, of course, a statue of himself, holding in one hand a lump of iron ore and in the other a scroll proclaiming a long list of his manufacturing achievements. I suppose the old oligarch is two and eighty and wishes to ennoble himself alongside famous ministers, military leaders, plutocrats, poets and authors, in one of the greatest cemeteries in Russia, his intended last resting place.'

'According to the police,' asserted Holmes, 'it was Lida Bezlukov's habit of a Monday morning to visit the grave of her late mother and place fresh flowers or some token of her respect beneath the headstone. Even in the depths of a Russian winter she would never waver from this routine, for she inherited from her mother Anna both her ravishing looks and a romantic temperament which inclined her towards music and poetry. It is said the vulgar statue of her father, the oligarch, repulsed her so much that she would often throw snowballs at it!'

'And the ransom demand,' Miss Perevin reminded us, wringing her hands. 'Oh, how awful, written in blood, explaining she would die unless the money was paid.'

'The gruesome note is, I think, questionable – animal or human blood. Of course, as Doctor Watson will confirm, my own researches to find alternatives for the old Guaialum test for haemoglobin were quite remarkable, but even so, under the microscope the identification of blood types remains a difficult science.'

'Oh, Mr Holmes, I should so like to visit the scene of the abduction for myself. The official police, Papa tells me, can be prejudiced against the wealthy classes, slow and indifferent in cases of crime.'

'They can be paid substantial bribes, of course,' remarked Holmes curtly, stepping across to the window to survey the snowy Moscow scene outside. 'But it so happens, Miss Perevin, Doctor Watson and I were about to take a visit to Novodevichiy Cemetery. You are most welcome to join our little excursion. We can lunch later at the Metropole's restaurant, if you feel so inclined.'

The russet red and white triple-domed gate-church of the intercession is situated along the south wall of Novodevichiy Convent, the entrance to the cemetery just wide enough to drive a hearse through.

The fog lifted, the startling glare of snow contrasting against the wintry grey sky of a Moscow afternoon. As we strode along the path, on either side of us elaborate tombs, impressive statuary and rows of snow-covered graves we came to an intersection and here, on a corner, was placed the newly constructed Bezlukov tomb, the fitting future resting place for the Iron King of Russia. Conspicuous was his replica cast in bronze, a giant of a fellow towering above all he surveyed. The military leaders, leading officials, the poets and the revered authors were dwarfed by this immense edifice.

Nearby was the much less ostentatious grave of

Anna, the late mother of Lida Bezlukov, a dignified, polished headstone bearing an integrated, tastefully tinted in memoriam photograph of the deceased, in life a handsome woman indeed.

My companion, smoking his briar-root pipe, fussed around the grave, prodding here and there with his silver-topped cane, thereafter turning his attention to the path.

'You will observe, my dear Watson,' said he, puffing on his pipe, 'the wheel ruts of a lightweight carriage crushing the surface of the frozen snow. Fortunately for us there was only a light fall of snow at the weekend and the narrow, crinkly furrows leave a discernable trail, leading from the gate-church of the intercession back here again to that grave further along where I am pointing. This morning the ground is frozen. We begin at the mother's grave. Firstly, isolate Lida Bezlukov's movements. I observe the Moscow police were here yesterday. They stomped about, smoked and compared notes wearing the standard issue, hefty, nail-studded clodhoppers, which *we can easily eliminate. Ah, bravo! See here, Nalèvo Naprano* – soles and heels consistent with ladies' winter footwear. I should say Lida Bezlukov wore a pair of ladies' boots similar to Miss Perevin's – fashionable and shapely Viktor-Karins. The trail leads ... Watson! Now this is highly irregular. Stoop down, old fellow. Mind yourself, Miss Perevin, have a care on the ice, it is decidedly slippery over here further up the path. Pray, what do either of you deduce?'

'A carriage drew up,' said I. 'We can discern she walked with an even step, *unhurried.*'

'And that bothers me,' replied Holmes, knocking out the ashes of his pipe, staring intently at the ground. 'From what we can gather, using the set of footprints as our guide, Lida Bezlukov is stood over by her mother's grave. A carriage approaches, not a hearse but a lightly sprung mourning coach with curtained windows. It stops over there, a little further down. Miss Bezlukov suspects nothing. A number of gentlemen pause, pretending to pay their respects at that grave further along with the marble statuary, portraiture and bronze-lettered sign recalling the transient life of young Grigory Shusky. She has her back turned, lost in grief, herself praying silently, perhaps talking softly to the spirit of her mother. Then they strike – at least they should strike fast and brutally hard, overpowering the beautiful daughter of the oligarch, perhaps with a mask soaked in chloroform, before dragging her along this path to the waiting mourning coach. In a very short time they are away, the horse and carriage trotting at a respectable pace towards the gate-church of the intercession. Being a Monday and deep winter, presumably Novodevichiy Cemetery is quiet and deserted. No grave spotters or visitors.'

'A mourning coach!' cried our young companion, clapping her mittens. 'The perfect means of deception. These evil torturers, strong-willed louts prepared to hustle her away and ruin her young life. Oh, forgive my tears, gentlemen, for in my heart I fear she is herself dead, murdered at the hands of her abductors, desperate to escape her ruthless captors, cut down like a wild dog. Why else should I have been witness to a visitation, her ghost lingering awhile on a Moscow street, clinging to this existence, unable to move on?'

'Contrary to your inclinations towards the mediumistic, else psychical, Miss Perevin, I should say these footprints show us clearly another chain of events entirely. I should, presuming the line of enquiry I outlined is correct, have expected a scuffle, a slithering about to gain purchase, heels dug into Monday's crisply packed snow, a brief struggle from Lida Bezlukov. Instead? Why Watson, look for yourself. It is ordered, sedate, it appears likely she walked across and stepped into the waiting coach. Does not that strike you as odd, Miss Perevin?'

'The footmarks are pressed very uniformly into the snow, it is true,' she admitted, wiping her cold nose before returning her hanky to her little silver bead purse and sniffing. 'But mightn't the chloroform have acted quickly?'

'Even so, why is there no rush of desperation, no aggression, no excitement about this?'

With a curl of his lip, Holmes kicked a loose shard of ice and sent it scuttling across the ground. Thereafter, much to our chagrin, tucking in his scarf and treading on a firmer crust of snow piled in small drifts along the edges of the cemetery path, he burst out laughing. He absently tapped the stem of his old briar-root pipe on the ridge of his nose.

'Excuse my prying, Miss Perevin. Apart from Olga you have a brother. Are they perchance employed in the banking sector? Your father is the director of Grand Financial, after all.'

'Both my sister and I attend Moskovskaya

Konservatoriya to study music. I am a cellist and Olga a promising pianist. Now, Dimitri, my brother, is an oaf, a nincompoop. He lives with Papa in Moscow at his town house, goes to work as a lowly novice clerk in the postal room at the bank, spends all his time staring out of the window, picking his nose, scribbling poetry, quite the idler. Poor exasperated Papa has given up on Dimitri inheriting his boardroom mantle, and is always threatening to disinherit him unless he gets off his backside and does something with his life.'

Holmes began chuckling again.

'I see no room for frivolity, sir,' cried Raisa, puzzled by my colleague's unaccountable behaviour. 'While we are alive and able to walk around and breathe the air of Moscow, Lida Bezlukov is either dead or cooped away in some filthy hole, a dark cellar, a lonely winter cabin used by trappers. Where is she, for goodness sake, Mr Holmes? Where was she taken in this cloak-and-dagger mourning coach of yours?'

'To Tverskaya, of course, a charming little tucked-away town house along a side street off the main avenue. *Kak proiti!* Number nineteen, isn't it?'

'Chto! Ya ne ponim ponimayu – that's Papa's address.'

'Precisely, Miss Perevin. Am I forgiven,' said he contritely, 'for filching your address book while we were changing into our fur coats earlier? I only wished to consult it briefly and you have my complete assurance it is safely returned to your purse, none the worse for its excursions.'

'Well, I must say – I mean, isn't that rather...'

'To continue, my dear Miss Perevin, it is not lost to me or Doctor Watson, and neither should it be to you, that all the evidence before us indicates no one was actually criminally abducted from Novodevichiy Cemetery; rather, it was an attempt, successful as it turned out, to hoodwink the police and Moscow's corps of press and wire agencies into making it *appear* that a definite, serious crime took place. The truth is much more prosaic. There were all along but three alternatives for us to consider:

1. She is tied up in some darkened hiding place, miserable and near death.
2. She has already departed this world and is a ghost, as you imply.
3. Happily, the more likely scenario, my dear Miss Perevin, is that she has entirely given her heart to a young Dimitri, and he to her, and she is presently occupying a spare room at the top of your papa's Moscow town house. Your father, the director of Grand Financial is too busy to notice there is a pretty intruder in his household, but she will not be there for too long, anyhow.'

'They intend to elope?'

'After purloining the ransom money, certainly! But not without risk. We can expect perhaps a large canvas bag containing the money discreetly left behind a tree in the park, but I am of the opinion the oligarch will comply, the Moscow police being kept out of the main business, of course, for he shall naturally not wish his beautiful, wayward daughter to be accidentally killed in some shoot-out, the result of a bungled operation to thwart the so-called kidnap gang.'

'My brother and her! Lida to become...'

'To be wed, exactly. Why not? And we only have to gaze upon that sculpture over there, the bronze statue of the Iron King gazing down at us so reproachfully, to understand what has occurred. Can you not hear him, Raisa? "You? Marry that postal clerk, Perevin, the son of that swine banker, who has no prospects or business acumen? I have no choice but to cut you off without a kopek, cut you out of my will. You shall not receive one single rouble while you remain infatuated by this ... this rascal. Marry him? Never!"

'But why does he refer to your papa as a swine? Because, my dear Miss Perevin, they have a long-standing and bitter feud going back many years, since the oligarch received better terms and a more favourable approach from a rival Moscow bank and withdrew considerable funds, his fortune in iron from the one, and transferred it to the latter, nearly causing Grand Financial to collapse. Your father, the director, required all his undoubted banking skills to avert a financial disaster. I learnt all of this, by the way, from that most informed of Muscovites, Mme Kalita, our general manager's secretary, after making discreet enquiries about your father's illustrious banking career. Is it really likely that your papa would approve of such a love match between his son and the daughter of the person he most despises in the world, the Iron King of Russia? Unlikely.'

'Thus our dreamy, nose-picking poet Dimitri, denizen of the post room, must use his wits. Their future happiness is put in jeopardy, which is intolerable,' said I.

'You make out Papa to be unfeeling and cruel,' complained our young lady friend, 'that he is a martinet ruling his family with a rod of iron and this is just not the case. I can assure you my oafish brother Dimitri is a most lazy and indolent fellow.'

'But far cleverer than any of you give him credit, for along with his future bride, Dimitri has masterminded a simple compromise of sorts. A means of outwitting both the banker and the oligarch and netting himself and Lida a considerable sum into the bargain.'

'But Mr Holmes, really...'

'The Moscow police... The forces of law and order, are they to be informed, the authorities alerted? Not a word, my dear Miss Perevin – let our love birds collect the loot and go off to Europe and enjoy themselves. The Iron King shall not pine over a deficit of a half million for long and your papa can fill a vacancy for a postal clerk, surely. Hello, why the bothersome expression?'

'Because ... because ... b-b-because it's all so unorthodox, Mr Holmes.'

'Ah, as Doctor Watson will himself concur, I pride myself on being a trifle unorthodox, Miss Perevin.'

Holmes straightened his fur hat and we began walking back the way we had come, the first flecks of a fresh fall of snow blowing about the cemetery.

In retrospect I should say this Russian case of 1898 provides the discerning reader with an insight into my colleague's remarkable ability to reason ahead of actual events and his analytical methods of deduction to solve a crime successfully.

The names Raisa and Olga Perevin will of course be familiar to lovers of classical music for the sisters are, as I write this account of my friend's adventures many years later, world famous performers on the concert platform, being a first rate cellist and recital pianist respectively.

9

The Plight of Lady Halliford

A solicitor acting on behalf of his client had by letter requested my colleague, Mr Sherlock Holmes, a consulting detective of world renown, to look into the distressing case of Lady Halliford.

Widely reported at the time was the somewhat sensational revelation that the widowed Lady Halliford of Beningbrough Hall, a red-brick mansion settled amongst the craggy moorlands of the Yorkshire Dales, had been lately committed to the care of an insane asylum after she was seen at dead of night wandering about the churchyard in nothing more than her nightdress, else oft-times all modesty forgotten, entirely naked, talking to the graves.

Her local physician, a medical man by the name of Derby, was of the opinion that the anniversary of the death of her husband, Lord Godfrey, in a tragic riding accident near Horton some years back, was partly the cause, but not entirely. She had recently been distressed due to morbid circumstances pressed upon her concerning the reinterment of her late mother due to a land subsidence in the churchyard.

Upon the morning of our visit the parson, the Rev. Stoddart, a corpulent and florid-faced fellow, forthright in his views and openly disdainful of outsiders, inserted a key and with a violent twist anticlockwise allowed us into the crypt. Inside was a low ceiling supported by squat, circular pillars.

'We store coke down here for our braziers, Mr Holmes.' The Rev. Stoddart paced between the rows of cobwebby shelves used to support coffins. 'Mr Ogden, our local coal and paraffin merchant, delivers a consignment of coke for use in autumn and winter months. Before the installation of the braziers, our remote church was fearfully cold and bitter, even to a hardy Yorkshireman such as myself. There is adequate space, and I am always careful the fuel is neatly heaped out of the way.'

'Hum, over here I observe a coffin in varying stages of rottenness. Brass handles and fitments cast by a T. Bucksworth of Kirkby. Presumably this scuffed receptacle belongs to Lady Halliford's recently exhumed mother Edna!'

'Aye, that is so, sir. Before her advantageous marriage Lady Margaret was plain Margaret Sharples, daughter of Edna. The family was fairly well-to-do and lived in the village.'

'Stoddart, I understood her ladyship was summoned over to the church from Beningbrough Hall because of an urgent matter pertaining to the fragile state of her late mother's coffin.'

'Of course. I was myself present, for Mr Ogden, while entering the crypt, noticed that the lid to her coffin had fallen onto the floor so it smashed.'

'Enabling all present to peer inside. And this is what all the bother is about, I take it.'

'Exactly, it is what was inside that made all of us get down on our knees and pray for forgiveness. Pray for the deliverance of our souls.'

'What do you make of this, Watson?'

'Most odd,' said I, brushing away a layer of dust from the skull of the old remains. 'I confess, in my opinion this looks more akin to the skeleton of a large hound. What's that dangling round its neck?'

'It's a silver amulet. I don't think under present ecclesiastical law we need bother too much about disturbing the remains of an animal, do you?'

'What is it – a dog tag?'

'Star signs. Decorative patterns around the perimeter depicting various astrological ascendants.'

'That is extraordinary,' said I. 'This coffin, according to the name plate, should contain Edna Sharples. Instead, we have the remains of what appears to be a large mastiff.'

'Just look at that jawbone, Watson, it possesses the most ferocious set of incisors.' My colleague was scouring the mouldy taffeta lining of the mother's coffin with his magnifying lens.

'There can only be one explanation,' announced the parson grimly.

'Oh, what is that?' asked my colleague, carefully examining the silver necklet between his fingers, studying each link minutely.

'My flock here in Beningbrough and I are of the opinion that the severe flooding and land subsidence last month in the graveyard were responsible for unearthing, resurrecting, if thou will, a mythical hound known in these parts for centuries as the Devil Dog of Blea Moor, the corpus of the mother after burial being somehow possessed of its evil shape-shifting form. I told her ladyship as much. I had little choice in the matter, for already Mr Ogden had spread the news about the opened coffin all round the village.'

'Was that not a trifle tactless, even unkind, to relate to her ladyship, considering her fragile state of mind over the anniversary of her husband's death?' asked Holmes. 'A cleric should, after all, be a compassionate soul.'

'The facts, sir, speak for themselves. The hellish hound, the Devil Dog of Blea Moor, is amongst us. I regret to tell thee, gentlemen, that mother Edna later in life was a vicious, foul-mouthed scold who bore no one any favours.'

'The facts remain unclear, Stoddart. You have assumed, wrongly in my opinion, that this coffin contains animal remains belonging to a mythical beast. May I refer you back to the reinterment.'

'A special service was held, I well recall. The old waterlogged grave was in a terrible state of repair since the flooding so we deemed it best to remove the mother's coffin to a dryer, more contained place. Her ladyship and I accompanied the remains in a lamplit procession across to the church. It seemed to me every stray dog in't village were barking and yowling.'

'A phantom dog – Beningbrough is presently alive and crackling with superstitious rumour, no doubt.'

'Thou choose to laugh, sir. Us Yorkshire folk

are to you, I suspect, but a rabble of primitives. Here, read for yourself.'

WILD BEAST AT BENINGBROUGH – FIVE PEOPLE ATTACKED

An invalid, Mary Cray, who lives in a cottage and as a rule sleeps with her bedroom window open, had her throat badly mauled last night by what the local police are describing as a wild animal – possibly escaped from some private sanctuary. Mr Tuffnell from the big house was adamant that none of his dogs were let out but the Alsatians were unusually agitated. Others in the village also noticed their pets behaving oddly, as if affected by some malign influence. Another person was viciously attacked last night and one person, a tramp, later taken to the hospital in Settle.

The school house is closed until further notice and armed estate workers who are searching the area, hoping to track down the animal, have warned members of the public to be especially vigilant and keep their pets indoors.

'A half-starved, ill-treated mongrel off its leash, running amok through the village, could just as easily be responsible,' said I.

After leaving the church, before removing to the town of Settle for luncheon, where my colleague had an appointment with Mr Fairclough, her ladyship's solicitor, Holmes and I sought out the local shop and I was amused while he charmed the lady behind the counter, at the same time asking some probing questions.

'*The Yorkshire Trumpet,* that most scintillating of

popular newspapers. Might I enquire whether it has a broad circulation?'

'T' paper boy, 'e delivers to ol' Mrs Griggsley, 'n' tha' ol' gossip Miss Toper and Mrs Ogden an' 'er little daughter 'oop coalman's cottage. That'll be one an' eight pence fer't thy *Times* 'nt baccy.'

'Notepaper, an envelope, and pen and ink if you please, madam. I must dash off a few words to our esteemed housekeeper, Mrs Hudson, back in London.'

'An illustrated postcard should be much more to her fancy,' said I. 'Shall I pick one from the rack, Holmes?'

'A note will suffice,' said he, cutting me dead. 'A first-class postage should reach her by the evening delivery. There! It's done and sealed.'

At Settle, a little grey and red market town nestling amongst the mountains in the vale of the Ribble, we enjoyed a fine luncheon of beefsteak and beer bitters at a hostelry along the High Street, not far from our hotel, thereafter going off in search of Lady Halliford's solicitor, Mr Fairclough of Fairclough and Grimthorpe, commissioner of oaths.

We were shown into a street-facing office; wood-panelled, with furniture of dark oak. A cheery fire blazed in the grate and a dear, sweet-natured Labrador curled sleepily in front of it. Mr Fairclough was a kindly, pinched-faced old legal man, full of polite platitudes and concern for our every comfort.

'Miss Biggs, a tray of tea and biscuits. Please feel free to smoke, gentlemen. Have you made much headway?'

Holmes lit his pipe and nodded. 'It is a dangerous business when a tiny, out-of-the-way Yorkshire village becomes notorious for harbouring the devil's dog in its church. I fancy this matter had better be cleared up quickly, Mr Fairclough. How is Lady Margaret bearing up, by the way?'

'She stubbornly refuses to speak to anyone, eats little and remains confined to her ward. The doctors are not optimistic. It is probable she will remain confined, perhaps for the rest of her life. Her ladyship is in a deep psychotic state of melancholy from which neither I nor anyone else can unburden her.'

'Blast Stoddart! He behaved insensitively, showing her the broken coffin, filling her with a feeling of guilt and mortification.'

'Yes, I agree his behaviour was questionable.'

'May I see the original letters you received from her brother and the parson?'

'Certainly, Mr Holmes. I have them here in my desk. I can have copies duplicated by my clerk, if you so wish.'

My companion took his time perusing the neatly written epistles sent locally.

My Dear Lady Halliford,
It pains me to inform you that due to continuous rain and flooding in this part of Yorkshire, a severe subsidence took place in the churchyard and your mother's grave was ruined, one whole side crumbling away. It is of course so very distressing but as your beloved mother always attended Sunday service and held dear our remote little church, her love and affection for this place

knowing no bounds, I wonder if it would be possible to reinter your mother in our church crypt, to save the bother of untold expense and workmen's invoices. The land is still sinking due to groundwater levels.

Your obedient servant,
The Rev. Arthur Stoddart (MA Oxon)

'Very straightforward,' muttered my companion, passing the first letter to me and studying the other letter from her ladyship's brother with interest.

Dearest Margaret,
So Mama is to be re-interred. Now that the anniversary of poor old Godfrey's death approaches, do remember he passed from this life doing what he loved best: riding with the hunt. It a pity Turpin fell heavily in the ditch but there we are. Chin up, old girl. Write soon.

Yours,
Sid

'Pray, does Sidney Sharples still live in Beningbrough?'

'After his father's death the butcher's business went downhill. There is now only one shop left in Yorkshire and that is in Hebden Bridge, where Sidney owns and manages Sharples Meat & Poultry. He earns a fair living, I daresay.'

'No history of debt or profligacy?'

'Sid is a true Yorkshireman, Mr Holmes – headstrong, hardworking, tight with his wallet. He likes his beer, pipe, brass bands and cricket. He would never dream of borrowing money off anybody, certainly not Lady Margaret, if that's what you're inferring. He usually visits the hall at Christmas but prefers his life in Hebden Bridge, I think.'

'Does he, indeed? Well, I am grateful for your time, Fairclough. Now I fear we must pry into the very epicentre of this sad case. Doctor Watson and I shall tomorrow morning press on by catching the train across the moors to Garsdale. Threshfield Asylum, isn't it? I shall require an urgent interview with her ladyship. I have a few contesting issues.'

'No visitors are permitted without first notifying the asylum master, Doctor Tatlock, in writing, Mr Holmes, at least a week or so prior to visiting a secure patient. They are very, very strict upon this so you had better leave me to arrange things.'

'Well, my dear Watson, tomorrow I quite fancy a little excursion on the Midland Railway Settle to Carlisle route. A train journey across the moors may prove a pleasant diversion. We shall consult my pocket Bradshaw's as to the train times in this remote region of Yorkshire. Good evening, Fairclough. I shall be in touch shortly.'

The next day, whilst our train rattled over the Ribblehead Viaduct at its own slow and unhurried pace towards Garsdale, with Whernside, the highest of the peaks in the distance, the broad, bleak and inhospitable perspective of craggy heath and moorland on either side, I recounted at length that the legend of the devil as a large dog is an old one, not just confined to Yorkshire but prevalent in the Fens.

'The original Black Shuck, Holmes, is a Norfolk

dog with a single eye that burns like a lantern. "Old Shock" as opposed to "Shuck" is a variety of Suffolk hound and a most horrific, ghostly dog was encountered at Bungay, Suffolk, in 1577.'

Holmes merely grunted.

'I should like to hear what you have to say about the silver amulet we found with the bones of the old mastiff,' said I. 'Was it of great value or antiquity?'

Leaning back on the cloth-covered seat, smoking his briar-root pipe, Holmes had a somewhat amused expression upon his pale, gaunt features.

'None of that, dear fellow. A long study under the lens revealed the legend "Made in Bradford – free with every copy of *The Yorkshire Trumpet*'. You know those infernal astrological stargazing issues that "tell your future", lighter efforts so beloved of editors of daily papers to ensnare its readers of the fairer sex.'

'Free with *The Yorkshire Trumpet!* Good gracious, Holmes, that means, all things considered, the bones in the exhumed coffin were simply exchanged, the mother Edna Sharples being replaced, say, by the skeleton of a large mastiff, the cheap necklace added merely for show.'

'Precisely, Watson. Our cocksure Yorkshireman evidently takes us for a couple of impressionable southerners. We are to believe this free gift to be capable of mystical powers, a talisman of some kind.'

'And the telegram you received from Mrs Hudson this morning at our hotel. I trust she is fit and well?'

'Oh, indeed, dear boy. I received a confirmation

of sorts, a past case of which I required certain details.'

My colleague puffed the more avidly upon his pipe, briefly consulting his pocket watch as to the correct time.

'Ah, we shall be arriving at Garsdale station shortly. The asylum, situated upon lonely Abbotside Common, is a twenty-minute trot by a hired dog cart, I'd venture to say.'

The heavy wrought-iron gates squealed open, presenting us with our first view of Threshfield Asylum. The old place was a granite and slate building with pitched roof, barred windows, a bell tower and tall brick chimney stacks.

'These secluded institutional places upon the moors are so vast and rambling, dear boy, that no one really has any idea what's going on, else who's coming and going.'

We abandoned our dog cart at the gates and trudged up the drive towards the imposing entrance porch. We waited for a time, dwarfed by an immense set of riveted double doors. I tugged the bell pull repeatedly.

A shutter snapped open. A pair of beady eyes both cunning and curious peered suspiciously through the grille.

'Who is it – laundry?'

'Brought the specialist with me,' said Holmes, stifling a yawn. 'One of the inmates contracted a fever.'

'Oh, that'd be Wilberforce,' came the grumpy response. 'The fool attempted to slice off his fingers last week and eat them.'

The vast, cathedral-like doors swung open and we were ushered inside, accosted by the smell of soapy water mopped well round. That, and the underlying odour of bodily filth.

'Ah, now I am reminded. Tatlock mentioned something about a specialist medical opinion being required. It is supposed the fellow's wounds became bacterially infected by the common house fly, of which, I regret to say, we have a great surfeit at present due to the uncommonly warm weather. I shall take you to see the asylum master and he shall direct you to the infirmary. All our visitors must be approved first by him.'

'Excellent. Tatlock is a most benevolent counsellor of the inmates, is he not? I have heard he is modern in his approach.'

'Oh he is, sir, he is. Such a wise and clever man. So efficient in the mortuary when he gets his scalpel and cuts a dead patient. This way if you please, sirs. Do be careful how you go; certain of our patients are allowed to wander about. Pay no heed if we encounter them, they are really quite jolly, but can without the slightest provocation behave outrageously and become dangerous so far as us "normals" are concerned.'

We were shown along a depressing labyrinth of corridors, walls painted duck green, the floor covered with what must have been acres and acres of shiny maroon dappled linoleum. Swing doors led to various wards. A slow-witted fellow with a scarred, shaved head came lumbering towards us grinding his teeth, pushing a laundry trolley.

'The mass murderer Cummings,' Worthington the orderly trilled. 'Oh, they are such "star turns", our inmates.'

We allowed him to pass.

'Got off the gallows on account of his insanity, lucky chap. Harmless, of course – lobotomised.'

We eventually came to a door with a sign upon it.

C. Tatlock, MSc, PhD, Asylum Master –
Private. No admittance.

The door was ajar. The orderly knocked.

'Yes, what is it Worthington?'

'Gentlemen to see you, sir.' Our guide, sensing nothing was amiss, chose to hurry off and leave us to it.

The pale and serious frock-coated individual busily writing up patient notes behind his imposing desk was, I should imagine, of an age of two and forty, with a prominent brow, long parted hair, a goatee beard and perfectly trimmed moustache above a firm mouth, giving him the look of a foreign professor or one of these faddish Viennese psychoanalysis who were then all the rage.

'May I ask what you people are doing here?' he wanted to know. 'How on earth did you get in here? My asylum is private and out of bounds to all but my staff and patients.'

'Ah,' Holmes answered, feigning confusion and removing his top hat. 'Forgive me, I thought you would have been notified by now. Did you not receive our letter, Doctor Tatlock?'

'I'm afraid I'm not with you.'

'Brains.'

The asylum master's jaw dropped.

'Lots of them.'

'I beg your pardon?'

'I'm so sorry, Doctor Tatlock, it appears there has been a monumental muddle. I wrote to say I should be visiting Garsdale with my friend Ernest Frogmorton, both of us enthusiasts of pathology from Cambridge, and that we should be travelling on the Settle-Carlisle railway to view your extensive collection of pickled brains, kept in jars over at the mortuary, I take it.'

'There are indeed many past inmates' brains on display, many of them dissected and floating in a solution of formaldehyde. You are most welcome to view these specimens. I can see you are both distinguished gentlemen up from Cambridge, and on this occasion I shall allow you one hour only to visit my mortuary. I am being lenient because of your connection to Cambridge, but I must emphasise we are normally out of bounds due to the extremely volatile and dangerous patients kept here at the asylum. You'd better hurry after Worthington, my head orderly, and ask him to take you over to the medical wing. Good day to you both, and I shall expect you off the grounds and on your way back to Settle Junction within the hour.'

My colleague cared nothing for Worthington, nor the medical wing, but pressed on regardless to the women's ward further along the corridor.

'There she is, Watson,' he whispered. 'Peep through the window partition. See her sat before the barred window? Poor Lady Halliford has come down in the world, all right. Stoddart has much to answer for. Both he and Doctor Derby presumably signed the necessary papers for her to be committed to Threshfield Asylum.'

'Well, old man, after our visit to the solicitor's office I am persuaded that the brother, Sidney, had something to do with all this. Could he not have conceivably tampered with the coffin? Is he to inherit the hall if she dies, or is deemed insane?'

'Her brother,' remarked my companion in that cold and contemplative way I knew so well, 'has nothing whatsoever to do with this. It is the once prosperous "King of Yorkshire Butchers", the father, Harry Sharples I shall be concentrating my own enquiries upon. Now, Watson, we must make a bolt for it, taking Lady Margaret to safer waters. Her incarceration is soon to be ended.'

Her ladyship's bath chair creaked and waned, a continuous rocking motion from a woman who appeared so wooden and unreceptive she could have been a lifeless doll magically transformed to human size. Holmes, infuriated by her ignoring him, shook her firmly by the shoulders, shook her so hard her eyelids fluttered open. Other patients on the ward under the same narcotic torpor seemed little concerned.

'Lady Halliford, your late father, Harry Sharples, apart from his commitments as a businessman, was a notable magistrate in Settle. A man was tried at the assizes and hanged for murdering a horse trader, Nathaniel Duckworth. The man was wrongly accused, as it turned out, of thieving a mare and beating the trader to death with an iron bar at the market place. He died a horrible, slow death, for the execution was bungled by the hangman and it took an age for him to die. Your father never forgave himself for providing the police with unsafe evidence, for he had poor eyesight and had mistaken the identity of the villain during the brawl. What was that man's name – the fellow's surname? I must hear it from your own lips, Lady Margaret, if I am to help you escape this barbaric confinement.'

She nodded and drew my colleague closer, whispering something inaudible to me in his ear. That was enough. Without further delay we hurried out of the ward, dragging the poor woman between us. Utilising a back kitchen entrance, thus avoiding any grey-coated orderlies prowling about, we half walked, half ran across the grounds to a patch of deciduous woodland whence we escaped onto the chalky track.

'Stay with Lady Margaret,' insisted Holmes. 'I shall dash round to the gates and fetch our dog cart. It is imperative we make a run across Abbotside Common for Garsdale station and fetch her ladyship to Settle as quickly as time will allow. Mr Fairclough and his wife shall be able to take care of her. A good hot meal and a loving home and friendly companionship shall improve her spirits immeasurably. We, on the other hand, my dear Watson, shall return to our hotel for a leisurely dinner and bed.'

Like a skittish fawn this poor woman, still wearing her obligatory asylum uniform of grey serge, a smock tied together at the back, so humiliating and ill-fitting, clung onto my arm and would not let go.

'God bless you both,' she uttered with a glimmer of a smile, 'for setting me free.'

'Your ordeal is at an end,' said I, drawing her

closer and comforting her.

We rose late the following morning to wet and windy weather, a dismal overcast day, angry storm clouds scudding across moorland above the town of Settle. Sheeting rain and a brisk wind howled across the rooftops and chimney pots, causing the window frames of our hotel room to shake and rattle. At breakfast, Holmes ate his ham and eggs with relish, and afterwards as we smoked our pipes in the dining room, he was pleased when a lengthy note arrived from Lady Halliford, who was feeling much better because she had received welcome news from Canada.

We eventually arrived at Beningbrough at around midday, travelling by hired horse and trap, and visited an isolated feudatory cottage in the village, set some distance back from the road, with a coal cart parked out front.

'Mr Ogden,' Holmes, knocked gently at the door of the stone cottage.

The coal merchant was at home and greeted us in a friendly way. The fellow was holding a yellow ferret in a cage, his young daughter close by gazing at us with childish wonderment and glee.

'Mary, go and play, that's a good little girl. So it's thee, Mr Holmes. Would you care for a cup of tea, gentlemen?'

'I shall desist for now, if you don't mind. We have more pressing issues to consider.'

'What be they?'

The view through the half-open door presented us with a glimpse of the homely hearth. The range creating a warm and cosy radiance, both convivial and welcoming, a child playing with her wooden donkey, while a scrawny collie dog stretched out on the hearth rug before his master's ill-sprung, worn-out old armchair.

'It was Harry Sharples, not his daughter, Lady Margaret, who helped put a rope around your father's neck, Mr Ogden. As that absurdly simple yet profound saying tells us, "two wrongs do not make a right". Her ladyship, I'm sure you'll be glad to know, has quit the constraints of Threshfield Asylum and is making a full recovery under the careful stewardship of her solicitor, Mr Fairclough, over at Settle.'

'What? I don't give a damn. Thou seest a wrong where there ain't 'un,' exclaimed the cottager, closing the door behind him so that we should not be overheard.

'On the contrary, I see a wrong, a worse wrong, and an even worse wrong, all of your own doing, Ogden. How could you come down so brutally hard on such a fragile, gentle creature as Margaret, already a pining widow? Oh, I realise from a youngster you have blamed the Sharples for your father being snatched away and cruelly hanged for a crime which he did not, as was later proven, commit. For this you have my every sympathy. But to allow one of your erstwhile badger-baiting companions to unleash an aggressive, half-starved lurcher to attack willy-nilly whom it pleased, to one night dig up the long decomposed remains of an immense mastiff and knowingly tamper with the mother's coffin – that, sir, is beneath contempt.'

'I'll admit to nowt, thou can'st prove nowt.

Begone, the pair of ye, and let me 'ave me lunch in peace.'

'Fortunately for you, Ogden, her ladyship informed me that she is to start a new life in Canada, with a dear and trusted close friend of Lord Godfrey's, person of impeccable lineage who has shown over the years, by way of voluminous correspondence, that he is prepared to take Margaret for his wife. This letter has filled her heart with renewed optimism and she will sell up and go abroad and join him at the next opportunity.'

'I admit to nowt, I did nowt,' the coal merchant shouted angrily, slamming the door in our faces. But there were tears in his eyes and Holmes and I heard a violent unrestrained sobbing from within.

Returning to London on the train I probed deeper, for I confess I was still unclear as to how Holmes reached certain of his conclusions and what first pointed the way to the local coal merchant being the culprit.

'You know, Watson,' said he, glancing up from the pages of *The Times* newspaper which he had been reading since our departure, 'the silver amulet, free with *The Yorkshire Trumpet*, offered on closer inspection certain unique possibilities. The chain's links, you see, had at some stage been reduced in number, altered so that the little necklet might fit the smaller, more petite neck of a child.'

'Mary,' said I, understanding at long last. 'The coal merchant's charming little daughter, who was at the door the morning we visited the cottage.'

'Just so. You will recall I was anxious to know

the circulation of *The Yorkshire Trumpet*. In a tiny remote village such as Beningbrough I suspected there would be few, for the *Yorkshire Post* and *Gazette* are by far the most popular dailies in this area. Two elderly women were mentioned, I believe, plus a third person.'

'Good gracious, Mrs Ogden, of course, and the fact she had a child – masterly! But the miscarriage of justice concerning the wrongly hanged man, how on earth did you deduce that?'

'Once I was clear who it was had tampered with the coffin, I realised that Ogden must be dreadfully put out about something, perhaps from his past. What possible reason would a chap have to go to so much trouble to hurt Lady Margaret? A deep-seated grudge, of course. We can safely assume the coalman could not believe his luck when the coffin of Edna Sharples, the mother of Lady Halliford, was placed in the crypt where the winter coke was stored. My memory, as you know, Watson, never fails me so far as criminality is concerned. I recalled a case of wrongful hanging some years ago, a man arrested in Settle, and merely requested Mrs Hudson look up an old file.'

'Indexed lists of cases going back the last twenty years or so under "O" for Ogden!' said I.

'Ha ha, Watson, you are yourself aware of my complicated filing system but nonetheless Mrs Hudson must be congratulated for such sterling efforts to locate the necessary facts I required at such short notice and wire me from the telegraph office at Baker Street accordingly.'

10

A Peculiar Slaying

Victoria Park, London's first public park, was opened in the heart of the East End in 1845, and upon a wintry morning in 1896 when the whole of London was for days in the grip of cold north-easterly winds from the Arctic, the streets and pavements treacherous and frozen over with dirty, compacted snow, it was my great good fortune to accompany my friend and erstwhile colleague Mr Sherlock Holmes, along with Inspector Lestrade, to that same 'Viccy' Park, as it was fondly referred to in those days by cockneys, to assist Scotland Yard in unravelling one of the most sensational murders yet encountered in the capital.

'Cor lummy, sir, h'ain't seen nuffink like it in all my time h'as a pleeceman,' observed a member of the local Mile End constabulary who stepped forward to greet us; a somewhat subdued crowd of morbid sightseers needed dispersing.

'Stand aside, Constable, this is Mr Sherlock Holmes and his companion Doctor Watson. Sergeant Fenlow, would you and your men be good enough to rope off this area and keep the gawpers and press people over by the drinking fountain.'

'Very well, Inspector. Modus operandi suits this bloomin' cold weather, don't it sir?' The sergeant of police along with a number of accompanying officers went about the work of sealing off that section of park. 'Come on you lot over there – back against them railings, let's be 'avin' yer, make it sharpish.'

The onlookers reluctantly turned on their heels and walked away, leaving the area free from their lingering, inquisitive stares.

The reader may be forgiven for thinking my forthcoming narrative to be concerned with a sequel to the Ripper murders of 1888, in some way linked to that debacle of Whitechapel, but this is not the case. There was no horribly mutilated corpse of a woman to be found splayed in the shrubbery, thankfully, although I confess Holmes and I were faced with an unusual enough sight as we trudged across the snowy green of Victoria Park that morning.

'Well, what do you make of it, gentlemen? I should value your opinion, Mr Holmes,' said Lestrade, clapping his gloves together to fend off the cold.

I recall being confronted by a large slab of ice, rectangular in shape, which contained the suspended frozen body of a fully clothed man who had evidently met his end by drowning in that same solid mass of water. Copious air bubbles were preserved, trapped in the ice for all and sundry to witness, the victim's features contorted in a hideous rictus of suffocation, revealing his final hapless, agonising struggle for life. Outstretched fingers clawed uselessly for purchase, desperate to find some means of escape.

'The block of ice is a devil of a puzzle,' said I, totally at a loss. 'How on earth did it get here, placed so prominently in the midst of the green for all to see?'

'Oh, indeed, Doctor Watson,' said Lestrade, passing round cigarettes. 'A patrolling constable doing his rounds could barely believe his eyes.'

'Pray, what time was the body discovered?' queried my companion, stooped low, peering curiously at the suspended corpse.

'The block of ice? Ten past four of the clock,' confirmed Lestrade. 'It was only on closer inspection the officer noticed the corpse frozen within. 'Course, the dead chap must have drowned, that much is clear, but how and where did the drowning occur? Certainly not in Viccy Park.'

'The gentleman is solidly encased in the very water responsible for his destruction. A novel touch, I must say,' exclaimed my colleague.

'Both daytime and night-time temperatures for the last week have been well below zero,' I pointed out.

'Allowing our cussed murderer to create and maintain what I should best describe as a "death sculpture" of his unfortunate victim preserved for public display in the park. A despicable business,' said Holmes.

'Despicable or not, it will be the devil's own job to defrost a corpse, to thaw this poor fellow out of his icy constraints. Well, well, I am waiting, Mr Holmes. Have you deduced anything of value to the case so far?' asked Lestrade.

'I am already forming a useful impression regarding the method of dispatch, certainly.'

'Don't hang about, share your views. I am the representative for Scotland Yard in this affair, after all.'

'I trust, Lestrade, you have noted that our gentleman is fully clothed, wears a winter overcoat tightly buttoned up, a copy of *The Sporting Times* poking out from one of the deep pockets.'

'I can see that, certainly.'

'Apart from the fact he was obviously a betting man, fond of the turf more seriously, this indicates to me he was taken completely by surprise and the murderer's intention was to drown him as quickly and efficiently as possible with the minimum of resistance, or need for restraints. We observe how the fellow attempted to twist round, the fingers of his left hand grasping for some means of purchase.'

'Go on, I can see you're onto something.'

'To be brief, I am of the opinion the victim was tripped or deliberately pushed into an oblong tank full of solidifying cold water, a heavy, cumbersome metal lid slammed directly on top of him, effectively sealing him in on every side, thus making all means of escape impossible. After a brief and futile struggle the shock of the icy immersion should have caused the heart to stop.'

'What a terrible way to die, trapped like that,' I remarked with feeling.

'Undoubtedly whoever killed him, Watson, had planned the strategy carefully beforehand. We must assume the guilty party had accomplices.'

'To transport this bloomin' weighty block of ice to Viccy Park would have required additional men and a horse and cart, surely,' said the inspector, puffing on his cigarette.

'Indeed.'

'But look here, Holmes,' said I, 'the laws of physics dictate you can't simply empty a tank full of frozen liquid like this. The sides should be virtually immovable. You can see how smooth and clear the surface is. The edges of the block of ice remain unscathed. The solid block of frozen water was not tipped out from the tank or chipped away to free it.'

'Bravo, a most astute observation, if I may say so, my dear Watson. We can but conjecture there might have been a removable base to the tank, or at some other location a system of hot water pipes incorporated into the design, or a number of flaming pitch torches were used to warm the metal up, to loosen the ice block sufficiently from its containment. Might I also draw your attention, Inspector, to the thick soles of the deceased gentleman's stout pair of walking shoes, impregnated as they are with sandy deposits and tiny particles of metal. I should say this person worked in an office in a factory, a foundry to be more precise, and spent some small time on the shop floor. Even without the benefit of a magnifying lens you will notice how smooth are the palms of the hands, the absence of healed scars consistent with a worker whose occupation takes him in daily close contact with a furnace or the forging of molten metal.'

'Well, I'm blowed,' ejaculated Lestrade, stamping on his cigarette, 'the mortuary wagon's arrived. About time.'

'Then we shall depart, inspector, for a little foray into the East End. Might Doctor Watson and I call on you later this afternoon at Scotland Yard?'

'I should be honoured, Mr Holmes. I shall be grateful for any further information useful to this murder enquiry. Good morning, gentlemen.'

For a while we paused for reflection and sat on a convenient park bench, smoking our pipes. I made pencil sketches in my notebook, a number of rough and ready diagrams that would help determine the mechanics of that blasted clever water tank device.

'The method of ejecting the solid mass of ice from the container totally eludes me, Holmes,' I confessed. My companion, who had been staring into the middle distance, proposed the following.

'For now we must neglect your container, Watson. We must search out a local foundry for I am convinced the murder was committed nearby and that the victim lived in the neighbourhood. There cannot be too many manufacturers hereabouts.'

'Now I've been thinking,' said I. 'The horse and cart utilised to transport the block of ice to Victoria Park is surely traceable. A flat-top wagon would have sufficed. Why Holmes, a brewer's dray should be ideal. Don't Tidbury & Neames have a brewery round here?'

'My dear fellow, I can't abide this "horse and cart" nonsense of yours. Walking over here I noticed a number of tracks, hardly visible due to the icy, slippery surface of the path, where the snow of the week previous has compacted. But enough to be going along with, certainly.'

'Oh, what tracks were those?'

'I counted four sets of perambulator wheels, India rubber treads, wire-spoked, the largest circumference wheel at the rear of each conveyance.'

'Hand-held carts?' I wondered out loud. 'A barrow?'

'Invalid carriages,' chuckled my colleague, puffing on his pipe the more fervently. 'It took four burly, immensely physically strong fellows to man-haul that block of ice atop of a sledge to Victoria Park.'

'Disabled folk – sledge!'

'Exactly.'

'But that's preposterous!'

'I surmise each of these energetic chaps was possessed of immense biceps and upper body strength attributable to a weightlifter, else an accomplished athlete. They should have thick necks and broad backs but none would have the use of their legs. The invalid carriages, I shall conjecture, were operated by twisting handles.'

'So they hauled the sledge through the streets to get here.'

'Absolutely. Oh, I grant you it must have been a queer expedition, proceeding cautiously, anxious to avoid the local populace and the prying eyes of the constabulary, but it could be done – *and was!* The effect of their combined labours proved both criminally original and startling visually, their efforts entirely justified to a warped way of thinking.'

'Baffling to Scotland Yard.'

'Undoubtedly, my dear Watson, although I confess I have not the slightest inkling as to why this gentleman in the overcoat was murdered. The method is more understandable, however.'

'Anyhow, it's time for action,' I insisted. 'Let's get walking, Holmes, which is surely preferable to sitting around in the cold all day.'

Quitting Viccy Park, we trudged along Grove Road to Bethnal Green, where we came across a small foundry business, Jariff & Co., tucked behind a yard. To me, the place was at once hideous, dirty and disagreeable. The din was unbearable as we walked inside, the forging, grinding and lathing of metal taking place in an atmosphere of intolerable heat amid the shouting of voices. There was a glazed structure to one side of the factory where was situated a lighted office. A fellow wearing a beige work coat indicated we should step inside so we could hear ourselves speak. It turned out he was the supervisor and he presented himself as both cordial and welcoming.

'Might I enquire,' asked Holmes, removing his hat and perching on the side of the desk, 'if any of your office staff have perchance failed to turn up for work this morning?'

'Why should that concern you, sir?'

'Oh, we are presently conducting a survey on behalf of the Salvation Army, statistics as to the prolificacy of winter deaths amongst the elderly and the poor at this time of year, and also absenteeism from the work place due to the common cold and chesty coughs.'

'Well, actually, let me see. Mr Jariff, the owner, has not come in – most odd as he is normally a stickler for punctuality and has never missed a day's work in his life. Yesterday he seemed to me in the peak of physical health.'

'Until now.'

'Just so.'

'Is he fond of wearing a tweed overcoat, well

buttoned up against the cold?'

'Mr Jariff does wear one of those, it so happens.'

'A racing man?'

'Oh, we all like a flutter on the horses, sir.'

'And your employer lives in the neighbourhood?'

'Chaney Street. His grandfather started the business. All the family have lived in Bethnal Green. Now sir, I must be getting on, we have an order of iron guttering to complete.'

'One more question, if I may. I couldn't help noticing you have one of those queer cranes that operates along the ceiling on special tracks. There is a new looking gantry suspended high above where we are now. Is it used for maintenance? Some men are up there painting it as we speak.'

'The gantry bridging the factory floor is used for maintenance of machinery, yes.'

'But the structure appears to me new and shiny, whereas your crane bears all the customary wear and usage one would expect.'

'In fact, there was last year an unfortunate accident. The old gantry had not been properly maintained or inspected for ages and a bolt sheared. Five men fell to the floor and that's an awful long way down, sir. One killed, four crippled for life. Mind you, Mr Jariff never lost no work time over the matter. Business went on as usual.'

'Great heavens,' said I. 'Was it never reported in the newspapers, commented upon by the press?'

'It's just an industrial accident, sir. Some poor worker in Britain gets killed or maimed for life, the public couldn't care less. The toffs and politicians even less than that.'

'But compensation was paid, surely.'

'Compensation? That's a dirty word so far as Mr Jariff is concerned. Do me a favour, we live in the real world. Mr Jariff would never dream of handing out compensation. I can assure you those poor devils received not one single farthing from the company. We used to see 'em come round here in their wheeled chairs, waiting for the owner to make an appearance so they could harangue him for a fair settlement. The police shoved 'em off in the end. They became a nuisance. Well, life goes on. Good day, gentlemen, keep up the good work for the Sally Army.'

This bleak and grossly negligent attitude in the work place made my blood boil. It rankled, as did the exploitation of children in the mills and coal mines, which I personally found loathsome. However, Holmes quickly brushed aside any arguments and there was no more talk of industrial accidents. Instead, he seemed to have a spring to his step and kept humming a damned tune.

'My dear Holmes, I've had enough of the East End for one day. Can't we head west for Baker Street? Mrs Hudson will have a good lunch on the table and I'm famished. If only it would snow or sleet or some damned such thing. Instead, the blasted weather's static, just this wretched grey sky and cold to contend with. Are we any nearer to finding out who put that chap in a block of ice, by the way?' My colleague was still humming that popular gaiety hall tune which I found frankly irritating.

'My dear fellow, I thought you realised. The person frozen in ice was none other than Mr Jariff.'

'Of course, Holmes, how utterly foolish of me. No wonder you're so cheerful, and these crippled chappies seeking compensation for their terrible injuries caused while working at his foundry put him there.'

'Precisely. Now, if I'm not mistaken there is nothing East End folk like better than a lunchtime drink at a public house. We have The Lighterman a little further up Duke Street, The Prince Albert on the corner and The Grapes near the Carlton Theatre in Bethnal Green High Street. Which is it to be, Watson, for I'll heartily wager our disabled chaps convene regularly at one of those hostelries. Why, upon a miserable cold day as today, the requirement for a warm, cheery fire and convivial companionship must be irresistible indeed.'

Holmes was correct. Barely had we entered the public bar of The Prince Albert filled with all the fug of pipe and cigarette smoke than he squeezed my arm, for a raucous group of disabled fellows were sat at a table in the far corner over by the window. A warmly felt cockney sing-song was in progress. A plump lady wearing a ridiculous flowery silk hat and feather boa was sat at the beer-stained piano striking the keys with podgy, clumsy fingers clubbing the tune to death. 'Roll out the barrel' was the punters' boisterous anthem. A chorus of inebriated ladies swayed happily on their chairs in time to the popular ditty. One of the crippled men singing at the top of his voice, so much the worse for drink, almost toppled out of his wheeled chair. Another disabled chap was brazenly supporting a pretty, slatternly wench upon his knee, sipping neat gin from a tumbler.

Holmes soon returned from the bar with a couple of halves of India pale ale. I had quite deliberately chosen a table within earshot of the crippled workers.

'That Jariff,' bellowed Holmes above the racket of off-key piano and croaking cockneys, 'his invoices are all wrong. He swindled me, I'm certain of it! I got overcharged for a set of water pipes.'

A drunken voice answered almost at once from the other table. 'Jariff – he'll trouble none of us n'more. We seen to 'im, all right. We done 'im – what's yer name, mister?'

'Briggs – Nathaniel Briggs,' lied my companion, raising his glass in a toast and grinning in a bovine, stupid way.

'Jariff,' roared another of the wheelchair crowd sitting nearest to us, slurring his words, incapable of proper speech, swigging bitter and slamming the beer mug so violently the glass cracked and a wave of foam drenched the polished surface of the table. 'You fink you was done by Jariff. Well, us lot got done worse. I ain't got the use of me legs n'more – all 'is flippin' fault.'

A man they called Alf slowly turned to face us. His wheeled chair creaked and the basket work, the wicker seat, sagged with his weight for he was a powerfully built chap. However, I can vouch there was no bonhomie or good fellowship in his eyes as he gave us a swift appraisal, only fear and suspicion.

'I fink you're the pleece.' A gun barrel rolled and clicked. He raised the old army weapon and pointed the barrel directly at us. 'I can smell a copper a mile off. Youse be plain clothes branch.

I'm right, ain't I?'

'Listen,' said Holmes kindly, 'I know how low you and your chums must feel. I can imagine the hatred and frustration. The fact you were cruelly denied compensation for your appalling injuries sustained at the foundry, the indignity of having to beg for fair play, to petition the owner for a morsel of pity. The judge at your trial may prove lenient. Let's talk sensibly.'

'Marfa,' he yelled to the lady pianist. 'Strike up the band, it's the fooneral march I'd quite fancy 'earin'. Nice an' slow like. Go orn, play it loud, my gal.' Alf twisted round, heading for the door. 'Keep out of my way the pair o' you plain clothes. I got business to attend to.'

The music started to play. The discordant, clumsy notes of that old faithful dirge proved strangely apt, for if he had only known it, he had but a short time to live.

'Alf's got a shooter,' someone screamed, 'and if 'e gets riled 'e'll use it.'

The pub door swung open, allowing in light and a freezing draught, and the powerfully built disabled man manoeuvred his wheeled chair with an awkward shove of his shoulders onto the first step, the rusty revolver still present on his lap. No sooner had he done so when, from what we could gather peering tentatively out of the window, police started to open fire from the top storey of the terraced house opposite. Alf died almost instantly in a hail of bullets, the distinctive tune of the funeral march accompanying the deadly racket that ensued. Eventually his battered, lopsided wheelchair keeled over and toppled down the steps, drunkenly spilling the ruined body of the once popular character, known and well-liked in the community of Bethnal Green, out onto the wintry, icy precinct of Drake Street.

The eerie pall of confused and shocked silence that hung over the public bar was palpable. The acrid stench of cordite and gun smoke still permeated the air. A woman's voice, polite and without undue emotion, broke the prevailing mood.

'It's him, Inspector Lestrade. Alfred Hornsby, the man who conspired with the others to murder my husband, the one who lived at Foundry Lane.'

I observed a dignified lady wearing a fashionable coat with a fur collar calmly cross the road and pause to dip the toe of her shoe in the widening pool of blood. This disgusted me.

'Lestrade, you oaf, you should have given the poor chap a chance,' I shouted angrily. 'Can't you see he's disabled? The bloody revolver's a war relic, it's rusted up.'

'Ah, Mr Holmes,' said he, smiling and entirely ignoring my argument. 'Mrs Jariff came forward this morning and identified the body of her late husband. She strongly suspected something was amiss when he did not return home yesterday evening after work. He had apparently been lured to Foundry Lane. In the courtyard of Alfred Hornsby's house we discovered, just as you had correctly surmised, Mr Holmes, an oblong water tank, together with a heavy weighted lid and a number of straw-wrapped torches and buckets of pitch used to warm the sides of the container when extricating the block of ice containing the body. Excuse me, my dear Mrs Jariff, I apologise profusely for becoming so bluntly forensic when referring to your late husband. Do you wish that a constable should accompany you back to your house? If so, you only have to ask.'

'Not at all, inspector. I trust the remainder of those idle loafers, those dirty good-for-nothings who assisted Hornsby in killing my husband so brutally, shall stand trial at the Old Bailey, and hang. I have nothing but contempt for them, Inspector.'

Acknowledgements

Thank you to all the team at Book Guild Publishing. I am also grateful to Amanda Payne for her valuable input.

The characters created by Sir Arthur Conan Doyle are used here by kind permission of Jonathan Clowes Limited on behalf of Andrea Plunkett, administrator of the Conan Doyle copyrights.

The publishers hope that this book has given you enjoyable reading. Large Print Books are especially designed to be as easy to see and hold as possible. If you wish a complete list of our books please ask at your local library or write directly to:

Magna Large Print Books
Magna House, Long Preston,
Skipton, North Yorkshire.
BD23 4ND